VIEW OF *BEAST*

"It's a pure terror-suspense-mystery story, complete with murder, detective, and surprise twist. But it is also so detailedly convincing a study in abnormal psychology, so admirably written with such complete realization of every character, that the most bitter antagonist of mystery fiction may be forced to acknowledge it as a work of art."

—Anthony Boucher
The New York TIMES

Who is Evelyn Merrick? Why is she persecuting wealthy Helen Clarvoe?

Paul Blackshear, Miss Clarvoe's financial advisor, looks for the answers and discovers *murder!*

BEAST IN VIEW

MARGARET MILLAR

INTERNATIONAL POLYGONICS, LTD.
NEW YORK CITY

for

BETTY AND JOHN MERSEREAU

best friends and

unseverest critics

Library of Congress Card Catalog No. 83-80874
ISBN 0-930330-07-2
Printed and Manufactured in the United States of America.

INTRODUCTION

Ghosts and goblins may frighten the average five-year old, and invasive creatures from outer space disturb his older sibs. Younger teenagers may titillate themselves with the idea of werewolves, the abominable snowman and Bigfoot. But the real fear of the average adult must be what lies in the deepest shadows of his own mind. It is the invasion from inner space, faces not quite seen, voices not quite heard. This is the stuff of nightmares. And while I was writing *Beast in View* I shared Helen Clarvoe's nightmare, when the face of fear became recognized and the voice one she knew well.

Near the end of the book my involvement with it was complete. I *was* Helen Clarvoe. Every sound was a threat, its volume exaggerated. The telephone no longer rang, it shrilled. People didn't talk, they screamed. A dog's bark would make me jump out of my chair. Creator and creation had become one. When this happens the result may be a strong and unforgettable book.

The experience of writing it had a profound effect on me. Readers' letters indicated it had the same effect on them. I was threatened with a libel suit, informed by a patient in a mental institution that at last she had found someone who really understood her, invited to join a coven of witches, asked to address a meeting of psychiatric social workers, and presented with the Mystery Writers of America Edgar Allen Poe award for best mystery of the year.

Beast in View was made into a play and a movie, and printed in a dozen languages throughout the world. Helen Clarvoe and I made a good team. I hope we never meet again.

Margaret Millar

Santa Barbara, Calif.
February, 1983

The voice was quiet, smiling. "Is that Miss Clarvoe?"

"Yes."

"You know who this is?"

"No."

"A friend."

"I have a great many friends," Miss Clarvoe lied.

In the mirror above the telephone stand she saw her mouth repeating the lie, enjoying it, and she saw her head nod in quick affirmation—*this lie is true, yes, this is a very true lie.* Only her eyes refused to be convinced. Embarrassed, they blinked and glanced away.

"We haven't seen each other for a long time," the girl's voice said. "But I've kept track of you, this way and that. I have a crystal ball."

"I—beg your pardon?"

"A crystal ball that you look into the future with. I've got one. All my old friends pop up in it once in a while. Tonight it was you."

"Me." Helen Clarvoe turned back to the mirror. It was round, like a crystal ball, and her face popped up in it, an old friend, familiar but unloved; the mouth thin and tight as if there was nothing but a ridge of bone under the skin, the dark brown hair clipped short like a man's, revealing ears that always had a tinge of mauve as if they were forever cold, the lashes and brows so pale that the eyes themselves looked naked and afraid. An old friend in a crystal ball.

She said carefully, "Who is this, please?"

"Evelyn. Remember? Evelyn Merrick."

"Oh, yes."

"You remember now?"

"Yes." It was another lie, easier than the first. The name meant nothing to her. It was only a sound, and she could not separate or identify it any more than she could separate the noise of one car from another in the roar of traffic from the

Boulevard three floors down. They all sounded alike, Fords and Austins and Cadillacs and Evelyn Merrick.

"You still there, Miss Clarvoe?"

"Yes."

"I heard your old man died."

"Yes."

"I heard he left you a lot of money."

"That's my business."

"Money is a great responsibility. I might be able to help you."

"Thank you, I don't require any help."

"You may soon."

"Then I shall deal with the problem myself, without help from any stranger."

"Stranger?" There was a rasp of annoyance in the repetition. "You said you remembered me."

"I was merely trying to be polite."

"Polite. Always the lady, eh, Clarvoe? Or pretending to be. Well, one of these days you'll remember me with a bang. One of these days I'll be famous, my body will be in every art museum in the country. Everyone will get a chance to admire me. Does that make you jealous, Clarvoe?"

"I think you're—mad."

"Mad? Oh no. *I'm* not the one who's mad. It's you, Clarvoe. *You're* the one who can't remember. And I know why you can't remember. Because you're jealous, you've always been jealous of me, you're so jealous you've blacked me out."

"That's not true," Miss Clarvoe said shrilly. "I don't know you. I've never heard of you. You're making a mistake."

"I don't make mistakes. What you need, Clarvoe, is a crystal ball so you can remember your old friends. Maybe I should lend you mine. Then you could see yourself in it, too. Would you like that? Or would you be afraid? You've always been such a coward, my crystal ball might scare you out of your poor little wits. I have it right here with me. Shall I tell you what I see?"

"No—stop this . . ."

"I see you, Clarvoe."

"No . . ."

"Your face is right in front of me, real bright and clear. But there's something wrong with it. Ah, I see now. You've been in an accident. You are mutilated. Your forehead is slashed open, your mouth is bleeding, blood, blood all over, blood all over . . ."

Miss Clarvoe's arm reached out and swept the telephone off the stand. It lay on its side on the floor, unbroken, purring.

Miss Clarvoe sat, stiff with terror. In the crystal ball of the mirror her face was unchanged, unmutilated. The forehead was smooth, the mouth prim and self-contained, the skin paper-white, as if there was no blood left to bleed. Miss Clarvoe's bleeding had been done, over the years, in silence, internally.

When the rigidity of shock began to recede, she leaned down and picked up the telephone and placed it back on the stand.

She could hear the switchboard operator saying, "Number please. This is the operator. Number please. Did you wish to call a number, *pulllease?*"

She wanted to say, *Give me the police,* the way people did in plays, very casually, as if they were in the habit of calling the police two or three times a week. Miss Clarvoe had never called the police in her life, had never, in all her thirty years, even talked to a policeman. She was not afraid of them; it was simply a fact that she had nothing in common with them. She did not commit crimes, or have anything to do with people who did, or have any crimes committed against her.

"Your number, please."

"Is that—is that you, June?"

"Why, yes, Miss Clarvoe. Gee, when you didn't answer, I thought maybe you'd fainted or something."

"I never faint." Another lie. It was becoming a habit, a hobby, like stringing beads. A necklace of lies. "What time is it, June?"

"About nine-thirty."

"Are you very busy?"

"Well, I'm practically alone at the switchboard. Dora's got flu. I'm warding off an attack of it myself."

Miss Clarvoe suspected from the note of self-pity in her voice and the slight slurring of her words that June had been warding off the flu in a manner not approved by the management or by Miss Clarvoe herself. She said, "Will you be going off duty soon?"

"In about half an hour."

"Would you—that is, I'd appreciate it very much if you'd come up to my suite before you go home."

"Why, is there anything wrong, Miss Clarvoe?"

"Yes."

"Well, gee whiz, *I* didn't do any . . ."

"I shall expect you here shortly after ten, June."

"Well, all right, but I still don't see what I . . ."

Miss Clarvoe hung up. She knew how to deal with June and others like her. One hung up. One severed connections. What Miss Clarvoe did not realize was that she had severed too many connections in her life, she had hung up too often, too easily, on too many people. Now, at thirty, she was alone. The telephone no longer rang, and when someone knocked on her door, it was the waiter bringing up her dinner, or the woman from the beauty parlor to cut her hair, or the bellboy, with the morning paper. There was no longer anyone to hang up on except a switchboard operator who used to work in her father's office, and a lunatic stranger with a crystal ball.

She had hung up on the stranger, yes, but not quickly enough. It was as if her loneliness had compelled her to listen; even words of evil were better than no words at all.

She crossed the sitting room and opened the French door that led on to the little balcony. There was room on the balcony for just one chair, and here Miss Clarvoe sat and watched the Boulevard three flights down. It was jammed with cars and alive with lights. The sidewalks swarmed with people, the night was full of the noises of living. They struck Miss Clarvoe's ears strangely, like sounds from another planet.

A star appeared in the sky, a first star, to wish on. But Miss Clarvoe made no wish. The three flights of steps that separated her from the people on the boulevard were as infinite as the distance to the star.

June arrived late after a detour through the bar and up the back staircase which led to the door of Miss Clarvoe's kitchenette. Sometimes Miss Clarvoe herself used this back staircase. June had often seen her slipping in or out like a thin, frightened ghost trying to avoid real people.

The door of the kitchenette was locked. Miss Clarvoe locked everything. It was rumored around the hotel that she kept a great deal of money hidden in her suite because she didn't trust banks. But this was a common rumor, usually started by the bellboys who enjoyed planning various larcenies when they were too broke to play the horses.

June didn't believe the rumor. Miss Clarvoe locked things up because she was the kind of person who always locked things up whether they were valuable or not.

June knocked on the door and waited, swaying a little, partly because the martini had been double, and partly because a radio down the hall was play-ing a waltz and waltzes always made her sway. Back and forth her scrawny little body moved under the cheap plaid coat.

Miss Clarvoe's voice cut across the music like a knife through butter. "Who's there?"

June put her hand on the door jams to steady herself. "It's me. June."

The door was unchained and unbolted. "You're late."

"I had an errand to do first."

"Yes, I see." Miss Clarvoe knew what the errand

was; the kitchenette already reeked of it. "Come into the other room."

"I can't stay only a minute. My aunt will . . ."

"Why did you use the back stairs?"

"Well, I didn't know exactly what you wanted me for, and I thought if it was something I'd done wrong I didn't want the others to see me coming up here and getting nosy."

"You haven't done anything wrong, June. I only wanted to ask you a few questions." Miss Clarvoe smiled, in a kindly way. She knew how to deal with June and people like her. One smiled. Even in an agony of fear and uncertainty, one smiled. "Have you ever seen my suite before, June?"

"No."

"Never?"

"How could I? You never asked me up before, and I didn't get my job here until after you moved in."

"Perhaps you'd like to look around a bit?"

"No. No thanks, Miss Clarvoe. I'm in kind of a hurry."

"A drink, then. Perhaps you'd like a drink?" One smiled. One coaxed. One offered drinks. One did anything to avoid being alone, waiting for the telephone to ring again. "I have some nice sherry. I've been keeping it for—well, in case of callers."

"I guess a nip of sherry wouldn't hurt me," June

said virtuously. "Especially as I'm coming down with flu."

Miss Clarvoe led the way down the hall into the sitting room and June followed, looking around curiously now that Miss Clarvoe's back was turned. But there was very little to see. All the doors in the hall were closed; it was impossible to tell what was behind any of them, a closet or a bedroom or a bathroom.

Behind the last door was the sitting room. Here Miss Clarvoe spent her days and nights, reading in the easy chair by the window, lying on the davenport, writing letters at the walnut desk: *Dear Mother: I am well . . . glorious weather . . . Christmas is coming. . . . My best to Douglas. . . . Dear Mr. Blackshear: Regarding those hundred shares of Atlas . . .*

Her mother lived six miles west, in Beverly Hills, and Mr. Blackshear's office was no more than a dozen blocks down the Boulevard, but Miss Clarvoe hadn't seen either of them for a long time.

She poured the sherry from the decanter on the coffee table. "Here you are, June."

"Gee, thanks, Miss Clarvoe."

"Sit down, won't you?"

"All right. Sure."

June sat down in the easy chair by the window and Miss Clarvoe watched her, thinking how much she resembled a bird, with her quick, hopping movements and her bright, greedy eyes and her bony little hands. A sparrow, in spite of the blonde hair and the gaudy plaid coat, a drunken sparrow feeding on sherry instead of crumbs.

And, watching June, Miss Clarvoe wondered for the first time what Evelyn Merrick looked like.

She said carefully, "I had a telephone call an hour ago, June, about nine-thirty. I'd be very— grateful for any information you can give me about the call."

"You mean, where it came from?"

"Yes."

"I wouldn't know that, Miss Clarvoe, unless it was long distance. I took three, four long distance calls tonight but none of them was for you."

"You recall ringing my room, though, don't you?"

"I don't know."

"Think hard."

"Well, sure, Miss Clarvoe. I *am* thinking hard, real hard." The girl screwed up her face to maintain the illusion. "Only it's like this, see. If someone calls and asks for Miss Clarvoe, then I'd remember it for sure, but if someone just asks for room 425, well, that's different, see."

"Whoever called me, then, knew the number of this suite."

"I guess."

"Why do you guess, June?"

The girl fidgeted on the edge of the chair, and her eyes kept shifting toward the door and then to Miss Clarvoe and back to the door. "I don't know."

"You said you *guessed*, June."

"I only meant I—I can't remember ringing 425 tonight."

"Are you calling me a liar, June?"

"Oh no, Miss Clarvoe, I should say not, Miss Clarvoe. Only . . ."

"Well?"

"I don't remember, is all."

They were the final words of the interview. There were no thank-you's or farewells or see-you-soon's. Miss Clarvoe rose and unlocked the door. June darted out into the corridor. And Miss Clarvoe was alone again.

Laughter from the next room vibrated against the wall and voices floated in through the open French door of the balcony.

"Honestly, George, you're a kick, a real kick."

"Listen to the girl, how cute she talks."

"Hey, for Pete's sake, who took the opener?"

"What do you think the good Lord gave you teeth for?"

"What the Lord gaveth, the Lord tooketh away."

"Dolly, where in hell did you put the opener?"

"I don't remember."

I don't remember, is all.

Miss Clarvoe sat down at the walnut desk and picked up the gold fountain pen her father had given her for her birthday years ago.

She wrote, Dear Mother: It has been a long time since I've heard from you. I hope that all is hell with you and Douglas.

She stared at what she had written, subconsciously aware that a mistake had been made but not seeing it at first. It looked so right, somehow: *I hope that all is hell with you and Douglas.*

I meant to say well, Miss Clarvoe thought. It was a slip of the pen. I hold no resentment against her. It's all this noise—I can't concentrate—those awful people next door . . .

"Sometimes you behave like an ape, Harry."

"Send down for some bananas, somebody. Harry's hungry."

"So what's so funny?"

"Take a joke, can't you. Can't you take a joke?"

Miss Clarvoe closed and locked the French doors.

Perhaps that's what the telephone call was, she thought. Just a joke. Just someone, probably someone who worked in the hotel, trying to frighten her a little because she was wealthy and because she was considered somewhat odd. Miss Clarvoe realized that these qualities made her a natural victim for jokers; she had become adjusted to that fact years ago, and behind-the-hand snickers no longer disturbed her the way they had in school.

It was settled, then. The girl with the crystal ball was a joke. Evelyn Merrick didn't exist. And yet the very name was beginning to sound so familiar that Miss Clarvoe was no longer absolutely certain she hadn't heard it before.

She pulled the drapes close across the windows and returned to her letter.

I hope that all is hell with you and Douglas.

She crossed out hell and inserted well.

I hope that all is well with you and Douglas. I don't, though. I don't hope anything. I don't care.

She tore the sheet of paper across the middle and placed it carefully in the wastebasket beside her desk. She had nothing really to say to her mother, never had, never would have. The idea of asking her for advice or comfort or help was absurd. Mrs. Clarvoe had none of these things to give, even if Helen had dared to ask.

The party in the next room had reached the stage of song. Down by the Old Mill Stream. Harvest Moon. Daisy, Daisy. Sometimes in close harmony, sometimes far.

A hot gust of anger and resentment swept through Miss Clarvoe's body. They had no right to make so much noise at this time of night. She would have to rap on the wall to warn them, and if that didn't work she would call the manager.

She started to rise but her heel caught in the rung of the chair and she fell forward, her face grazing the sharp edge of the desk. She lay still, tasting the metallic saltiness of blood, listening to the throbbing of the pulse in her temples and the panic beat of her heart.

After a time she pulled herself to her feet and moved slowly and stiffly across the room toward the mirror above the telephone stand. There was a slight scratch on her forehead and one corner of her mouth was bleeding where the underlip had been cut by a tooth.

. . . *"I have a crystal ball. I see you now. Real bright and clear. You've been in an accident. Your forehead is gashed, your mouth is bleeding. . . ."*

A cry for help rose inside Miss Clarvoe's throat. Help me, someone! Help me, mother—Douglas—Mr. Blackshear . . .

But the cry was never uttered. It stuck in her throat, and presently Miss Clarvoe swallowed it as she had swallowed a great many cries.

I am not really hurt. I must be sensible. Father always boasted to people how sensible I am. Therefore I must not become hysterical. I must think of something very sensible to do.

She went back to her desk and picked up her pen and took out a fresh sheet of note paper.

Dear Mr. Blackshear:

You may recall that at my father's funeral you offered to give me advice and help if the occasion should ever arise. I do not know whether you said this because it is the kind of thing one says at funerals, or whether you sincerely meant it. I hope it was the latter, because the occasion, you may have already inferred, has arisen. I believe that I have become the victim of a lunatic. . . .

CHAPTER 2

. . . It is distressing to me to have to confide these sordid details to anyone. I do not lightly cast my burdens on other people, but since you gave my late father such expert counsel, I would very much appreciate your advice in the situation I have described to you.

If you would be so kind as to telephone me when you receive this letter and let me have your opinion in the matter, I would be extremely grateful. I intend, of course, to express my gratitude in more practical terms than words.

Yours very truly,
Helen Clarvoe

The letter was delivered to Mr. Blackshear's office and then sent on to his apartment on Los Feliz because he had gone home early. He no longer appeared regularly at his office. At fifty, he was retiring gracefully, by degrees, partly because he could afford to, but mostly because boredom had set in, like a too early winter. Things had begun to repeat themselves: new situations reminded him of past situations, and people he met for the first time were exactly like other people he'd known for years. Nothing was new any more.

Summer had passed. The winter of boredom had set in and frost had formed in the crevices of Blackshear's mind. His wife was dead, his two sons had married and made lives of their own, and his friends were mostly business acquaintances whom he met for lunch at Scandia or the Brown Derby or the Roosevelt. Dinners and evening parties were rare because Blackshear had to rise long before dawn in order to be at his office by 6 o'clock when the New York stock exchange opened.

By the middle of the afternoon he was tired and irritable, and when Miss Clarvoe's letter was delivered he almost didn't open it. Through her father, who had been one of Blackshear's clients, he had known Helen Clarvoe for years, and her constrained prose and her hobbled mind depressed him. He had never been able to think of her as a woman.

She was simply Miss Clarvoe, and he had a dozen or more clients just like her, lonely rich ladies desiring to be richer in order to take the curse off their loneliness.

"Damn the woman," he said aloud. "Damn all dull women."

But he opened the letter because on the envelope, in Miss Clarvoe's neat, private-school backhand, were the words Confidential, Very Important.

> . . . Lest you think I am exaggerating the matter, I hasten to assure you that I have given an exact account both of the telephone call and my subsequent conversation with the switchboard operator, June Sullivan. You will understand, I am sure, how deeply shocked and perplexed I am. I have harmed no one in my life, not intentionally at any rate, and I am truly amazed that someone apparently bears me a grudge. . . .

When he had finished reading the letter he called Miss Clarvoe at her hotel, more from curiosity than any desire to help. Miss Clarvoe was not the kind of woman who would accept help. She existed by, for, and unto herself, shut off from the world by a wall of money and the iron bars of her egotism.

"Miss Clarvoe?"

"Yes."

"This is Paul Blackshear."

"Oh." It was hardly a word, but a deep sigh of relief.

"I received your letter a few minutes ago."

"Yes. I—thank you for calling."

It was more like the end of a conversation than the beginning. Somewhat annoyed by her reticence, Blackshear said, "You asked me for advice, Miss Clarvoe."

"Yes. I know."

"I have had very little experience in such matters, but I strongly urge you to . . ."

"Please," Miss Clarvoe said. "Please don't say anything."

"But you asked me . . ."

"Someone might be listening."

"I have a private line."

"I'm afraid I haven't."

She must mean the girl, June Sullivan, Blackshear thought. Of course the girl would be listening, if she wasn't busy elsewhere; Miss Clarvoe had probably antagonized her, or, at the very least, aroused her curiosity.

"There have been new developments." Miss Clarvoe's voice was guarded. "I can talk about them only in the strictest privacy."

"I see."

"I know how busy you are and I hate to impose on you, but—well, I must, Mr. Blackshear. I *must*."

"Please go on." Behind her wall of money, behind her iron bars, Miss Clarvoe was the maiden in distress, crying out, reluctantly and awkwardly, for help. Blackshear made a wry grimace as he pictured himself in the role of the equally reluctant rescuer, a tired, detached, balding knight in Harris tweeds. "Tell me what you want me to do, Miss Clarvoe."

"If you could come here to my hotel, where we can talk—privately . . ."

"We'd probably have more privacy if you came over here to my apartment."

"I can't. I'm—afraid to go out."

"Very well, then. What time would you like me to come?"

"As soon as you can."

"I'll see you shortly, then, Miss Clarvoe."

"Thank you. Thank you very much. I can't *tell* you how . . ."

"Then please don't. Good-bye."

He hung up quickly. He didn't like the sound of Miss Clarvoe's gratitude spilling out of the telephone, harsh and discordant, like dimes spilling out of a slot machine. The jackpot of Miss Clarvoe's emotions—*thank you very much.*

What a graceless woman she was, Blackshear thought, hoarding herself like a miser, spending only what she had to, to keep alive.

Although they communicated quite frequently by letter, he hadn't seen her since her father's funeral the previous year. Tall, pale, tearless, she had stood apart from the others at the grave; her only display of feeling had been an occasional sour glance at the weeping widow, Verna Clarvoe, leaning on the arm of her son Douglas. The more tears her mother shed, the more rigid Helen Clarvoe's back had become, and the tighter her lips.

When the services were over, Blackshear had approached Miss Clarvoe, aware of her mute suffering.

"I'm sorry, Helen."

She had turned her face away. "Yes. So am I."

"I know how fond you and your father were of each other."

"That's not entirely accurate."

"No?"

"No. I was fond of him, Mr. Blackshear, not he of me."

The last time he saw her she was climbing stiffly into the back seat of the long black Cadillac that was used to transport the chief mourners, Mrs. Clarvoe, Helen and Douglas. They made a strange trio.

A week later Blackshear received a letter from Miss Clarvoe stating that she had moved, permanently, to the Monica Hotel and wished him to handle her investments.

The Monica was the last place in the world he would have expected Miss Clarvoe to choose. It was a small hotel on a busy boulevard in the heart of Hollywood, and it catered not to the quiet solitary women like Miss Clarvoe, but to transients who stayed a night or two and moved on, minor executives and their wives conducting business with pleasure, salesmen with their sample cases, advertising men seeking new accounts, discreet ladies whose names were on file with the bellhops, and tourists in town to do the studios and see the television shows. All the kinds of people Miss Clarvoe would ordinarily dislike and avoid. Yet she chose to live in their midst, like a visitor from another planet.

Blackshear left his car in a parking lot and crossed the street to the Monica Hotel.

The desk clerk, whose name plate identified him as G. O. Horner, was a thin elderly man with protuberant eyes that gave him an expression of intense interest and curiosity. The expression was false. After thirty years in the business, people meant no more to him than individual bees do to a beekeeper. Their differences were lost in a welter of statistics, eradicated by sheer weight of numbers. They came and went; ate, drank, were happy, sad, thin, fat; stole towels and left behind toothbrushes, books, girdles, jewelry; burned holes in the furniture, slipped in bathtubs, jumped out windows. They were all alike, swarming around the hive, and Mr. Horner wore a protective net of indifference over his head and shoulders.

The only thing that mattered was the prompt payment of bills. Blackshear looked solvent. He was smiled at.

"Is there anything I can do for you, sir?"

"I believe Miss Clarvoe is expecting me."

"Your name, please."

"Paul Blackshear."

"Just a moment, sir, and I'll check."

Horner approached the switchboard, walking softly and carefully, as if one of his old enemies had scattered tacks on the floor. He talked briefly to the girl on duty, hardly moving his mouth. The girl looked over her shoulder at Blackshear with sullen curiosity and Blackshear wondered if this was the June Sullivan Miss Clarvoe had mentioned in her letter.

Blackshear returned her stare. She was an emaciated blonde with trembling hands and a strained white face, as if the black leech of the earphone had already drawn too much blood.

Horner bent over her but the girl leaned as far away from him as she could and started to yawn. Three or four times she yawned and her eyes began to water and redden along the upper lids. It was impossible to guess her age. She could have been a malnourished twenty or an underdeveloped forty.

Horner returned, his fingers plucking irritably at the lapels of his black suit. "Miss Clarvoe didn't leave any message down here, sir, and her room doesn't answer."

"I know she's expecting me."

"Oh, certainly, sir, no offense intended, I assure you. Miss Clarvoe frequently doesn't answer her telephone. She wears ear plugs. On account of the traffic noises, a great many of our guests wear . . ."

"What is the number of her suite?"

"Four-twenty-five."

"I'll go up."

"Certainly, sir. The elevators are to your right."

While he was waiting for an elevator, Blackshear glanced back at the desk and saw that Horner was watching him; he had lifted his protective veil of indifference for a moment and was peering out like an old woman from behind a lace curtain.

Blackshear disappeared into the elevator and Mr. Horner lowered his net again, and let the lace curtain fall over his thoughts: *That suit must have cost a hundred and fifty dollars. . . . These con men*

*always put up a good appearance. . . . I won-
der how he's going to take her and for how
much. . . .*

Miss Clarvoe must have been waiting behind the
door. It opened almost simultaneously with Black-
shear's knock, and Miss Clarvoe said in a hurried
whisper, "Please come in."

She locked the door behind him, and for a few
moments they stood looking at each other in silence
across a gully of time. Then Miss Clarvoe stretched
out her hand and Blackshear took it.

Her skin was cool and dry and stiff like parch-
ment, and there was no pressure of friendliness, or
even of interest, in her clasp. She shook hands
because she'd been brought up to shake hands as a
gesture of politeness. Blackshear felt that she dis-
liked the personal contact. Skin on skin offended
her; she was a private person. The private I, Black-
shear thought, always looking through a single key-
hole.

The day was warm for November, and Black-
shear's own hands were moist with sweat. It gave
him a kind of petty satisfaction to realize that he
must have left some of his moisture on her.

He waited for her to wipe her hand, surrepti-
tiously, even unconsciously, but she didn't. She

merely took a step backward and two spots of color appeared on her high cheekbones.

"It was kind of you to go to all this trouble, Mr. Blackshear."

"No trouble at all."

"Please sit down. The wing chair is very comfortable."

He sat down. The wing chair was comfortable enough but he couldn't help noticing that it, like all the other furniture in the room, was cheap and poorly made. He thought of the Clarvoe house in Beverly Hills, the hand-carved chairs and the immense drawing room where the rug had been especially woven to match a pattern in the Gauguin above the mantel, and he wondered for the dozenth time why Miss Clarvoe had left it so abruptly and isolated herself in a small suite in a second-rate hotel.

"You haven't changed much," Blackshear lied politely.

She gave him a long, direct stare. "Do you mean that as a compliment, Mr. Blackshear?"

"Yes, I did."

"It is no compliment to me to be told that I haven't changed. Because I wish I had."

Damn the woman, Blackshear thought. You couldn't afford to be nice to her. She was unable to accept a compliment, a gift of any kind; they seemed to burn her like flaming arrows and she had to pluck them out and fling them back with vicious accuracy, still aflame.

He said coldly, "How is your mother?"

"Quite well, as far as I know."

"And Douglas?"

"Douglas is like me, Mr. Blackshear. He hasn't changed either. Unfortunately."

She approached the walnut desk. It bore no evidence of the hours Miss Clarvoe had spent at it. There were no letters or papers visible, no ink marks on the blotter. Miss Clarvoe did not leave things lying about. She kept them in drawers, in closets, in neat steel files. All the records of her life were under lock and key: the notes from Douglas asking for money, her bank statements and canceled checks, gardenia-scented letters from her mother, some newspaper clippings about her father, an engraved wedding invitation half torn down the middle, a bottle of sleeping pills, a leash and harness with a silver tag bearing the name Dapper, a photograph of a thin awkward girl in a ballet dress, and a sheaf of bills held together by a gold money clip.

Miss Clarvoe picked up the sheaf of bills and handed it to Blackshear.

"Count it, Mr. Blackshear."

"Why?"

"I may have made a mistake. I get—flustered sometimes and can't concentrate properly."

Blackshear counted the money. "A hundred and ninety-six dollars."

"I was right, after all."

"I don't understand."

"Someone has been stealing from me, Mr. Blackshear. Perhaps systematically, for weeks, perhaps just once—I don't know. I do know that there should be nearly a thousand dollars in that clip."

"When did you discover some of it was missing?"

"This morning. I woke up early while it was still dark. There was some argument going on down the hall, a man and a woman. The woman's voice reminded me of the girl on the telephone, Evelyn Merrick, and I—well, it upset me. I couldn't go back to sleep. I began to wonder about Miss Merrick and when—whether I would hear from her again and what she hoped to get out of me. The only thing I have is money."

She paused, as if giving him a chance to contradict her or agree with her. Blackshear remained quiet. He knew she was wrong but he didn't feel that anything could be gained, at this point, by stating it: Miss Clarvoe had another thing besides money which might interest a woman like Evelyn Merrick, and that was the capacity to be hurt.

Miss Clarvoe continued quietly. "I got up and took a pill and went back to sleep. I dreamed of her—Evelyn Merrick. I dreamed she had a key to my suite and she let herself in, bold as brass. She was blonde, coarse-looking, made up like a woman of the streets—it's so vivid, even now. She went over to my desk and took my money. All of it." Miss Clarvoe stopped and gave Blackshear a long direct stare. "I know such dreams mean nothing, except that I was disturbed and frightened, but as soon as I woke up again I unlocked my desk and counted my money."

"I see."

"I told you about the dream because I wanted to make it clear that I had a *reason* for counting the money. I don't usually do such a thing. I'm not a miser pouring over a hoard of gold."

But she spoke defensively, as if someone in the past had accused her of being miserly.

"Why do you keep such a large amount of cash in your room?" Blackshear said.

"I need it."

"Why?"

"For—well, tips, shopping for clothes, things like that."

Blackshear didn't bother pointing out that a thousand dollars would cover a lot of tips, and the black jersey dress Miss Clarvoe was wearing indicated that her shopping trips were few and meager.

The silence stretched out like tape from a roller until there seemed no logical place to cut it.

"I like to have money around," she said, finally. "It gives me a feeling of security."

"It should give you the opposite."

"Why?"

"It makes you a target."

"You think that's what Evelyn Merrick wants from me? Only money?"

He realized from her stressing of the word "only" that she, too, suspected other factors were involved.

"Perhaps," he said. "It sounds to me like an extortion racket. It may be that the woman means to frighten you, to harass you, until you are willing to pay her to be left alone. It may be, too, that you'll never hear from her again."

Miss Clarvoe turned away with a little sighing sound that whispered of despair. "I'm afraid. I'm afraid sometimes even to answer the phone."

Blackshear looked grave. "Do you know more than you're telling me, Helen?"

"No. I wrote everything in my letter to you, every word that was spoken. She's—she's crazy, isn't she, Mr. Blackshear?"

"A little off-balance, certainly. I'm no specialist

in these matters. My business is stocks and bonds, not psychoses."

"You have no advice for me, then?"

"I think it would be a good idea if you took a vacation. Leave town for a while. Travel. Go some place where this woman can't find you."

"I have no place to go."

"You have the whole world," Blackshear said impatiently.

"No—no." The world was for couples, for lovers, for husbands and wives, mothers and daughters, fathers and sons. Everywhere in the world, all the way to the horizon, Miss Clarvoe saw couples, like her mother and father, and, now, Douglas and her mother, and the sight of them spread ice around her heart.

"England," Blackshear was saying. "Or Switzerland. I'm told St. Moritz is very lively in the wintertime."

"What would I do in such a place?"

"What do other people do?"

"I don't really know," she said seriously. "I've lost touch."

"You must find it again."

"How does one go about finding things that are lost? Have you ever lost anything, Mr. Blackshear?"

"Yes." He thought of his wife, and his endless

silent prayers when she was dying, his bargains with God: take my eyes, my arms, my legs, take anything but leave me Dorothy.

"I'm sorry," Miss Clarvoe said. "I didn't realize —I'd forgotten . . ."

He lit a cigarette. His hands were shaking with anger and remembered grief and sudden loathing for this awkward woman who did everything wrong, who cared for no one and gave nothing of herself even to a dog.

"You asked me for advice," he said with no trace of emotion. "Very well. About the missing money, you'll have to report that to the police. Whether you like it or not, it's your duty as a citizen."

"Duty." She repeated the word after him, slowly, as if it had a taste that must be analyzed, a flavor pungent with the past: castor oil and algebra and unshed tears and hangnails and ink from leaky pens. Miss Clarvoe was a connoisseur. She could pick out and identify each flavor, no matter how moldy with age.

"As for the woman, Evelyn Merrick, I've already given you my advice. Take a vacation. There are certain disordered persons who get a kick out of making anonymous phone calls to strangers or people they know slightly."

"She gave me her name. It wasn't an anonymous call."

"It was as far as you're concerned. You don't know her. You've never heard of her before. Is that right?"

"I think so. I'm not sure."

"Do you ordinarily remember people well— names, faces, conversations?"

"Oh yes." Miss Clarvoe gave a nod of bitter satisfaction. "I remember them."

Blackshear got up and looked out of the window at the traffic below. After-five traffic, with everyone hurrying to get home, in all directions; to Westwood and Tarzana, to Redondo Beach and Glendale, to Escondido and Huntington Park, to Sherman Oaks and Lynwood. It was as if the order had gone out to evacuate Hollywood and the evacuation was taking place with no one in command but a single traffic cop with a tin whistle.

Blackshear said, over his shoulder, "You're not good at taking advice."

"What you suggest is impossible. I can't leave Los Angeles right now, for personal reasons." She added vaguely, "My family."

"I see. Well, I'd like to help you but I'm afraid there isn't anything I can do."

"There is."

"What?"

"Find her."

He turned, frowning. "Why?"

"I want to—I must see her, talk to her. I must rid myself of this—uncertainty."

"Perhaps the uncertainty is in yourself, Helen. Finding a stranger may not help you."

She raised her hand in an autocratic little gesture as if she meant to silence him. But almost immediately her hand dropped to her side again and she said, "Perhaps not. But you could try."

"All I have to go on is a name."

"No. There's more than that. Remember what she said, that one of these days she'd be famous, her —her body would be in every art museum in the country. That must mean that she poses for artists, she's a model."

"Models are a dime a dozen in this town."

"But it at least gives you a place to start. Aren't there such things as model booking agencies?"

"Yes."

"You could try there. I'll pay you, of course. I'll pay . . ."

"You're forgetting something."

"What?"

"I'm not for hire."

She was quiet for a moment. "Have I offended you by mentioning money? I'm sorry. When I offer to pay people, I don't mean it as an insult. It's simply all I have to offer."

"You have a low opinion of yourself, Helen."

"I wasn't born with it."

"Where did you get it?"

"The story," she said, "is too long to tell, and too dull to listen to."

"I see." But he didn't see. He remembered Clarvoe as a tall, thin, quiet-mannered man, obviously fond of and amused by his frilly little wife, Verna. What errant chromosomes or domestic dissensions had produced two such incongruous children as Helen and Douglas, Blackshear could not even guess. He had never been intimate with the family although he'd known them all since Helen was in college and Douglas was attending a military prep school. Once in a while Blackshear was invited out to the house for dinner, and on these occasions the conversation was conducted by Verna Clarvoe who would chatter endlessly on the I—me—my level. Neither of the children had much to say, or, if they had, they had been instructed not to say it. They were like model prisoners at the warden's table, Douglas, fair-skinned and fragile for his age, and Helen, a caricature of her father, with her cropped brown hair and bony arms and legs.

Shortly after Clarvoe's death, Blackshear had been surprised to read in the society page of the morning paper that Douglas had married. He had been less surprised when a notice of annulment followed, on the legal page, a few weeks later.

"I know what you are thinking," Miss Clarvoe said. "That I should hire an experienced investigator."

Nothing had been further from his thoughts but he didn't argue. "It seems like a good idea."

"Do you know of anyone?"

"Not offhand. Look in the yellow pages."

"I couldn't trust a stranger. I don't even tr—" Her mouth closed but her eyes finished the sentence: I don't even trust you. Or mother, or Douglas. Or myself.

"Mr. Blackshear," she said. "I . . ."

Suddenly, her whole body began to move, convulsively, like that of a woman in labor, and her face was tortured as if she already knew that the offspring she was going to bear would be deformed, a monster.

"Mr. Blackshear—I—Oh, God . . ."

And she turned and pressed her forehead against the wall and hid her face with her hands. Blackshear felt a great pity for her not because of her tears but because of all the struggle it had taken to produce them. *The mountain labored and brought forth a mouse.*

"There, there, don't cry. Everything's going to be all right. Just take it easy." He said all the things that he'd learned to say to his wife, Dorothy, whenever she cried, words which didn't mean anything in themselves, but which fulfilled Dorothy's need for attention and sympathy. Miss Clarvoe's needs were deeper and more obscure. She was beyond the reach of words.

Blackshear lit another cigarette and turned to the window and pretended to be interested in the view, a darkening sky, a dribble of clouds. *It might rain tonight—if it does, I won't go to the office in the morning—maybe the doctor was right, I should retire altogether—but what will I do with the days and what will they do to me?*

He was struck by the sudden realization that he was in his way as badly off as Miss Clarvoe. They had both reached a plateau of living, surrounded by mountains on the one side and deep gorges on the other. Blackshear had at one time scaled the mountains and explored the gorges, Miss Clarvoe had not done either; but here they were, on the same plateau.

"Helen . . ." He turned and saw that she had left the room.

When she returned a few minutes later, her face was washed and her hair combed.

"Please excuse me, Mr. Blackshear. I don't often make a fool of myself in public." She smiled wryly. "Not such a *damned* fool, anyway."

"I'm sorry I upset you."

"You didn't. It was—the other things. I guess I'm an awful coward."

"What are you afraid of, the thief or the woman?"

"I think they're the same person."

"Perhaps you're interpreting your dream too literally."

"No." Unconsciously, she began to rub her forehead, and Blackshear noticed that it bore a slight scratch that was already healed over. "Do you believe that one person can influence another person to—to have an accident?"

"It's possible, I suppose, if the suggestion is strong enough on the part of the first person, and if it coincides with a desire for self-punishment on the part of the second person."

"There are some things you can't explain by simple psychology."

"I suppose there are."

"Do you believe in extrasensory perception?"

"No."

"It exists, all the same."

"Perhaps."

"I feel—I feel very strongly—that this woman means to destroy me. I *know* it. If you like, call it intuition."

"Call it fear," Blackshear said.

She looked at him with a touch of sadness. "You're like my father. Nothing exists for you unless you can touch or see or smell it. Father was tone-deaf; he never knew, in all his life, that there was such a thing as music. He always thought that when people listened to music they were pretending to hear something that wasn't really there."

"It's not a very good analogy."

"Better than you think, perhaps. Well, I won't keep you any longer, Mr. Blackshear. I appreciate your taking time out to come and see me. I know how busy you are."

"I'm not busy at all. In fact, I've practically retired."

"Oh. I hadn't heard. Well, I hope you enjoy your leisure."

"I'll try." What will you do with the days? he asked himself. Collect stamps, grow roses, sit through double features, doze in the sun on the back porch, and when you get too lonely, go to the park and talk to old men on benches. "I've never had much leisure to enjoy. It will take practice."

"Yes," Miss Clarvoe said gently. "I'm afraid it will."

She crossed the room and unlocked the door. After a moment's hesitation, Blackshear followed her.

They shook hands again and Blackshear said, "You won't forget to report the missing money to the police?"

"I won't forget to do it, Mr. Blackshear. I will simply *not* do it."

"But why?"

"The money itself isn't important. I sit here in my room and get richer without even raising my hand. Every time the clock ticks I'm richer. What does eight hundred dollars matter?"

"All right, then, but Evelyn Merrick matters. The police might be able to find her for you."

"They might, if they bothered to look."

Blackshear knew she was right. The police would be interested in the theft but there wasn't the slightest evidence that Evelyn Merrick was the thief. And as far as the phone call was concerned, the department received dozens of similar complaints every day. Miss Clarvoe's story would be filed and forgotten, because Evelyn Merrick had done no physical harm, had not even voiced any definite threats. No search would be made for the women unless he, Blackshear, made it himself.

I could do it, he thought. It isn't as if I'd be investigating a major crime where experience is necessary. All I have to do is find a woman. That shouldn't require anything more than ordinary intelligence and perseverance and a bit of luck. Finding a woman is better than collecting stamps or talking to old men on benches in the park.

He felt excitement mounting in him, followed by the sudden and irrational idea that perhaps Miss Clarvoe had contrived the whole thing, that she had somehow tricked or willed him into this reversal of his plans. *"Do you believe in extrasensory perception, Mr. Blackshear?"* "No."

No? He looked at her. She was smiling.

"You've changed your mind," she said, and there was no rising inflection of doubt in her voice.

CHAPTER 3

The following afternoon, after spending the morning at the telephone, Blackshear arrived at the establishment advertised in the yellow pages of the Central Los Angeles phone book as the Lydia Hudson School of Charm and Modeling. It was one of two dozen similar schools listed, differing only in name, location and degree of disregard for the laws of probability: We will make you a new person. . . . Hundreds of glamorous jobs awaiting our graduates. . . . We guarantee to improve your personality, poise, posture, make-up, figure, and mental outlook. . . . Walk and talk in beauty, our staff will teach you. . . .

Miss Hudson performed her miracles on the second floor of a professional building on Vine Street. The outer office was a stylized mixture of glass brick and wrought iron and self-conscious young women in various stages of charm. Two of them were apparently graduates; they carried their professional equipment in hatboxes, and they wore identical expressions, half-disillusioned, half-alert, like commuters who had been waiting too long for their train and were eyeing the tracks for a handcar.

They spotted Blackshear, and immediately began an animated conversation.

"You remember Judy Hall. Well, she's *finally* engaged."

"No! How did that happen?"

"I wouldn't *dare* to guess. I mean, her methods are pretty stark, aren't they?"

"They have to be. She's let herself go terribly in the past year. Did you notice her complexion? And her posture?"

"It isn't her posture that's so bad. It's her figure."

"I bet Miss Hudson could do wonders . . ."

Walk and talk in beauty, our staff will teach you.

Blackshear approached the reception desk and

the commuters stopped talking. Another train had passed without stopping.

"I have an appointment to see Miss Hudson. The name is Blackshear."

The receptionist's eyelids drooped as if from the weight of her mascara. "Miss Hudson is in Conversation Class at the moment, Mr. Blackshear. Will you wait?"

"Yes."

"Just have a seat over there."

She undulated across the room, walking in beauty, and disappeared behind a frosted glass door marked Private. A minute later a short woman with hair the color of persimmons and a mouth to match came out of the same door. She didn't undulate. She walked briskly with her shoulders back and her head thrust forward at a slightly aggressive angle, as if she expected to be challenged by a high wind or a disgruntled client.

"I'm Lydia Hudson." Her voice was incongruously soft and pleasant, with a faint trace of a New England accent. "Sorry to keep you waiting, Mr. Blackshear."

"You didn't."

"I was rather surprised by your phone call. You sounded so mysterious."

"Let's say mystified, not mysterious."

"Very well." She smiled a professional smile, without disturbing her eyes. "You're not a policeman, are you, Mr. Blackshear?"

"No."

"Maybe you're a lawyer, and the Merrick girl is a long-lost heiress. That would be fun."

"It would."

"But that's not it, eh?"

"No."

"It never is." Miss Hudson glanced at the two models who were making a noble pretense of not listening. "Your call hasn't come through yet, girls. Sorry."

One of the models put down her hatbox and started across the room. "But, Miss Hudson, *you* said be here at two and here we . . ."

"Patience, Stella. Patience and poise. One moment of distemper can be as damaging to your skin as two éclairs."

"But . . ."

"Remember, you're a *graduate* now, Stella. You can't afford to behave like a freshman." To Blackshear, she added softly, "Come into my office. We can't talk here in front of these morons."

Miss Hudson's office was artfully devised for the acquisition of new students. On each side of the desk where she sat was a lamp with a pink shade that flattered her complexion and made her hair look almost real. The other side of the room, reserved for prospective clients, was illuminated from the ceiling with fluorescent rods that gave a dead white light, and two of the walls were decorated with full length mirrors.

"This is our consultation room," Miss Hudson said. "I never give the girls any personal criticism. I simply let them study themselves in the mirrors and *they* tell *me* what's wrong. That way, it makes for a more pleasant relationship and better business. Please sit down, Mr. Blackshear."

"Thanks. Why better business?"

"I often find that the girls are much harder on themselves than I would be. They expect more, you see?"

"Not quite."

"Well, sometimes a very pretty girl comes in and I can't find anything the matter with her at all. But *she* can, because she's probably comparing herself to Ava Gardner. So, she takes my course." Miss Hudson smiled dryly. "Results guaranteed, naturally. Cigarette?"

"No thanks."

"Well, now you know as much about my business as I do. Or," she added, with a shrewd glance, "as much as you care to, eh?"

"It's very interesting."

"Sometimes the whole thing makes me sick, but

it's a living, and I've got three kids to support. The youngest is fourteen. When I get her through college or married off to some nice steady guy, I'm going to retire. I'm going to loll around the house all day in a bathrobe and bedroom slippers and I'm never going to open another jar of face cream as long as I live, and every morning when I get up I'm going to look in the mirror and chortle myself silly over a new wrinkle and another gray hair." She paused for breath. "Don't mind me. I'm only kidding. I think. Anyway, you didn't come here to listen to my blatting. What do you want to know about this Evelyn Merrick?"

"Everything you can tell me."

"It won't be much. I only saw her once and that was a week ago. She read my ad in the *News* offering a free consultation for a limited time only, and in she came, sat in the same chair you're sitting in now. A scrawny brunette very poorly dressed and made up like a tart. Pretty impossible, from a professional point of view. She had one of those Italian boy haircuts gone to seed. They're supposed to look casual, you know, but actually they require a lot of expert care. And her clothes . . ." Miss Hudson stopped sharply. "I hope she's not a friend of yours?"

"I've never seen her."

"Why do you want to find her, then?"

"Let's stick with the long-lost heiress story," Blackshear said. "I'm beginning to like it."

"I always have."

"You gave her the free consultation?"

"I did the usual thing, tried to put her at ease, called her by her first name and so on. Then asked her to stand up and walk around and watch herself in the mirror and tell me what she thought needed correction. Ordinarily the girls are embarrassed at this point, and sort of giggly. She wasn't. She acted—well, odd."

"In what way?"

"She just stood there looking into the mirror, without making a sound. She seemed fascinated by herself. I was the one who was embarrassed. . . ."

"Walk around a bit, Evelyn."

The girl didn't move.

"Are you satisfied with your posture? Your skin? How about your make-up?"

She didn't speak.

"It is our policy to let our prospective students analyze themselves. We cannot correct faults that the student doesn't admit having. Now, then, would you say that you are perfectly happy about your figure? Take a good honest look, fore and aft."

Evelyn blinked and turned away. "The mirror is distorted and the lights are bad."

"They are not bad," Miss Hudson said, stung. "They are—realistic. We must face facts before altering them."

"If you say so, Miss Hudson."

"I say so, I— How old are you, Evelyn?"

"Twenty-one."

She must consider me a fool, Miss Hudson thought. "And you want to be a model?"

"Yes."

"What kind?"

"I want to pose for artists. Painters."

"There's not much demand for that kind of . . ."

"I have good breasts and I don't get cold easily."

"My dear young woman," Miss Hudson said with heavy irony. "And what else can you do besides not get cold easily?"

"You're making fun of me. You simply don't understand."

"Understand what?"

"I want to become immortal."

Miss Hudson lapsed into a stunned silence.

"I couldn't think of any other way to do it," the girl said. "And then I saw your ad, and the idea came to me suddenly, suppose someone paints me, a really great artist, then I will be immortal. So you see, it makes sense, if you think about it."

Miss Hudson didn't care to think about it. She

had no time to worry about immortality; tomorrow was bad enough. "Why should a young woman like you be concerned about death?"

"I have an enemy."

"Who hasn't?"

"No, I mean a real enemy," Evelyn said politely. "I've seen her. In my crystal ball."

Miss Hudson looked at the cheap rayon dress stained at the armpits. "Is that how you make your living, telling fortunes?"

"No."

"What do you work at?"

"Just at the moment I'm unemployed. But I can get money if I need it. Enough to take your course."

"You understand we have a waiting list," Miss Hudson lied.

"No. No, I thought . . ."

"I shall be most happy to put your name on file." And leave it there. I want no part of your immortality. Or your crystal ball. "How do you spell your last name?"

"M-E-R-R-I-C-K."

"Evelyn Merrick. Age, 21. Address and phone number?"

"Well, I'm not sure. I'm moving out of my present place tomorrow, and I haven't decided just where I'll go."

No address, Miss Hudson wrote on her memo

pad. Good. It will give me the perfect excuse for not calling her.

"I'll phone you when I get settled," Evelyn said. "Then you can tell me if you have an opening."

"It might be quite some time."

"I'll keep trying anyway."

"Yes," Miss Hudson said dryly, "I believe you will."

"I'll call you, say, a week from today?"

"Listen to me a minute, Evelyn. If I were you, I'd reconsider this modeling business, I'd . . ."

"You are not me. I will call you in a week. . . ."

"The week was up yesterday," Miss Hudson told Blackshear. "She didn't call. I don't know whether I'm glad or sorry."

"I think," Blackshear said, "that you ought to be glad."

"I guess I am. She's a real mimsy, that one. God knows my girls aren't mental giants, not one of them has an I.Q. that would make a decent basketball score. But they're not really *screwy*, like her. You know what I wonder, Mr. Blackshear?"

"No."

"I wonder what she saw in that mirror when she stood there half-hypnotized. What did she see?"

"Herself."

"No." Miss Hudson shook her head. "*I* saw herself. She saw somebody else. Gives you the creeps, doesn't it?"

"Not particularly."

"It does me. I felt sorry for her. I thought, suppose it was one of my kids—suppose something happens to me before they're safe and grown-up, and they're cast out into . . . Well, we won't go into that. Very depressing. Besides, I'm healthy and I drive carefully. Also, I have a sister who's perfectly capable of taking over the kids if anything happened to me. . . ." In sudden fury, Miss Hudson reached out and slapped the fragile mauve and white desk with the palm of her hand. *"Damn* that girl! You go along for years, doing your best, not worrying about dying, and then something like this happens. Some screwball comes along with a bunch of crazy ideas and you can't get them out of your head. It's not fair. Damn her hide. I'm sorry I tried to help her."

Blackshear raised his brows. "How exactly did you help her, Miss Hudson?"

"Maybe I didn't. But I tried. I could tell she was broke, so I gave her the name of a man. I thought he might give her an odd job to tide her over until she came to her senses if any."

"What kind of job?"

"Posing. He's an artist, a good one, too, which means he has to teach to make ends meet. He uses live models in his classes, not just pretty girls, but all kinds and shapes and sizes. I figured it wouldn't do any harm to send Evelyn over there. He might take a fancy to her earlobes or her big toe or something. Moore's a stickler for details."

"Moore?"

"Harley Moore. His studio is on Palm Avenue, just off Sunset near Santa Monica Boulevard."

"Has she actually done any posing, do you know?"

"She said she had. She said she'd done some work for Jack Terola. He's a photographer, ten or twelve blocks south of here. I don't know much about him except that he pays pretty well. He does photo illustrations for one of those confession magazines—you know, where the wife is standing horrified watching her husband kiss his secretary, or the young Sunday school teacher is being assaulted in the choir loft—that sort of thing. My youngest kid reads them all the time. It drives me crazy trying to stop her. Stuff like that gives kids the wrong idea about the world—they get to thinking all secretaries get bussed by the boss and all Sunday school teachers are assaulted in choir lofts. Which isn't true."

"I hope not."

"Well, there you are."

Blackshear wasn't exactly sure where he was. But he knew where he was going.

The means to charm were apparently more profitable than its ends: Miss Hudson could afford glass bricks and mahogany paneling; Terola's place was a long narrow stucco building between a one-way alley euphemistically named Jacaranda Lane and a rickety three-story frame house converted into apartments. Black stenciling on the frosted glass window read:

PHOTOGRAPHIC WORKSHOP

JACK TEROLA, PROPRIETOR

PIN-UP MODELS · LIFE GROUPS FOR AMATEURS
AND PROFESSIONALS · RENTAL STUDIOS FOR ART GROUPS

Come in Any Time

Blackshear went in. In spite of the rows of filing cabinets and the samples of Terola's work which lined the walls, the office still looked like what it had been originally, somebody's front parlor. Near one end of the room was a dirty red-brick fireplace which had a desolate and futile appearance, as if it had become, from long disuse, a mere hole in the wall which a careless workman had forgotten to plaster over. To the right of the fireplace was a curtained alcove. The curtains were not drawn and Blackshear could see part of the interior: a brown leather chair, the seat wrinkled with age, a day bed partly covered with an old-fashioned afghan, and above it, the stenciled front window. The alcove reminded Blackshear of his childhood in the Middle West—all the best people had had a "sun porch," which was indescribably hot in the summer and equally cold in the winter and no good for anything at all except social prestige.

Terola's sun porch seemed to be not a mark of prestige but a sign of necessity. The day bed was obviously used for sleeping; a dirty sheet dribbled out from under the afghan and the pillow was stained with hair oil.

There was no one in sight, but from behind the closed door at the other end of the room came sounds of activity, the scraping of equipment being moved across a wooden floor, the rise and fall of voices. Blackshear couldn't distinguish the words but the tones were plain enough. Somebody was giving orders and somebody else wasn't taking them.

He was on the point of knocking on the closed door when he noticed the printed sign propped against the typewriter of Terola's desk: FOR ATTENTION, PLEASE RING.

He rang, and waited, and then rang again, and finally the door opened and a young girl came out, wearing a printed-silk bathrobe. She wore no make-up and her face glistened with grease and moisture. Water dripped from the ends of her short black hair and slid down her neck, and the damp silk of the bathrobe clung to her skin.

She seemed unconcerned. "You want something?"

"I'd like to speak to Mr. Terola."

"He's busy right now. Sit down."

"Thank you."

"I'm supposed to be drowning but Jack can't get the water right. It's supposed to be Lake Michigan, see."

Blackshear nodded politely to indicate that he saw.

"Jack's a sucker for drowning scenes," the girl added. "Me, I like to stay dry. The way I look at it is, I could just as easy been stabbed. All this fuss trying to make like Lake Michigan. Don't you want to sit down?"

"I'm perfectly comfortable."

"Well, all right. You here on business?"

"In a way. My name is Paul Blackshear."

"Pleased to meet you. I'm Nola Rath. Well, I better get back now. You want a magazine to read?"

"No, thanks."

"You may have quite a wait. If Jack gets this shot

right he'll be out here in a jiffy, but if he don't, he won't."

"I'll wait."

"I could just as easy been stabbed," the girl said. "Well, I'll tell Jack you're here."

She left behind a trail of water drops and the smell of wet hair.

Nola Rath. Blackshear repeated the name to himself, wondering how old the girl was. Perhaps twenty-five, only a few years younger than Helen Clarvoe, yet a whole generation seemed to separate the two. Miss Clarvoe's age had very little to do with chronology. She was a middle-aged woman because she had had nothing to keep her young. She was the chosen victim, not only of Evelyn Merrick, but of life itself.

The thought depressed Blackshear. He wished he could forget her but she nagged at his mind like a broken promise.

He looked at his watch. Three-ten. A wind had come up. The curtains of Terola's alcove were blowing in and out and the cobwebs in the fireplace were stirring, and somewhere in the chimney there was a fidgeting of mice.

"You wanted to see me?"

Blackshear turned, surprised that he had not heard the opening of the door or the sound of footsteps.

"Mr. Terola?"

"That's right."

"My name's Blackshear."

They shook hands. Terola was in his early forties, a very thin, tall man with an habitual stoop as if he were trying to scale himself down to size. He had black bushy brows that quivered with impatience when he talked, as if they were silently denying the words that came out of the soft feminine mouth. Two thin parallel strands of iron-gray hair crossed the top of his bald pate like railroad ties.

"Just a minute." Terola walked over to the alcove and drew the curtains irritably. "Things are in a mess around here. My secretary's home with the mumps. Mumps, yet, at her age. I thought they were for kids. Well, what can I do for you, Blackshear?"

"I understand you employ, or have employed, a young woman called Evelyn Merrick."

"How come you understand that?"

"Someone told me."

"Such as who?"

"Miss Merrick used your name as a reference when she went to apply for training as a model. She claimed she had done some work for you."

"What kind of work?"

"Whatever kind you had to offer," Blackshear

said, attempting to conceal his impatience. "You do quite a bit of—shall we call it art work?"

"We shall and it is."

"Have it your way. Do you remember Miss Merrick?"

"Maybe I do, maybe I don't. I'm not answering a lot of questions unless there's a good reason. You got a good reason, Mr. Blacksheep?"

"Blackshear."

"It's not that I don't want to co-operate, only I kind of like to find out first who I'm co-operating with, in what and for why. What's your business, mister?"

"I'm an investment counselor."

"So?"

"Let's say that there's an estate to settle and Evelyn Merrick may get a piece of it."

Terola spoke tightly, barely moving his mouth, as if he was afraid there might be lip-readers around peering in through the curtains of the alcove or the chinks in the chimney: "The kind of piece that babe gets won't come out of any estate, mister."

"She came here, then?"

"She came. Gave me a hard-luck story about a dying mother, so I let her have a couple of hours' work. I'm a sucker for dying mothers, just so's they don't change their minds and stay alive, like mine did."

"Did the Merrick girl give you any trouble?"

"I don't take trouble from chicks like that. I bounce them out on their ear."

"Did you bounce her?"

"She got nosey. I had to."

"When was this?"

"Couple of weeks ago, maybe less. When they get nosey, they get bounced. Not," he added with a wink, "that I have anything to hide. I just don't like snoopers. They get in my hair, what's left of it."

"What else did she do besides snoop?"

"Oh, she had some screwy idea about me making her immortal. At first I figured she was kidding and trying for a laugh. I have a pretty good sense of humor so I laughed, see? She got sore as hell. If you want the truth, I don't think she's playing with all her marbles."

"Exactly what kind of work did you give Evelyn Merrick?"

"She posed."

"For you personally? Or for one of your 'art' groups?"

"What difference does it make?"

"It might make a lot of difference to me."

"How so?"

"If she posed for you, for a magazine story layout, you might give me a print of the picture. If she worked with your art group, I don't think you will."

Terola ground out the stub of his cigarette in an ashtray. "I never give away prints."

"What do you do, peddle them?"

"Peddle is a very nasty word. You'd better leave before I push it back down your throat."

"I didn't realize what a sensitive fellow you were, Terola."

"I don't want any trouble with your kind. Blow."

"Thank you for the information."

Terola opened the door. "Go to hell."

Blackshear walked down the alley and got into his car. It was the first time in thirty years that he'd been close to having a fight and the experience aroused old memories and old fears and a certain primeval excitement. His hand on the ignition key was unsteady and anger pressed on his eyeballs like iron thumbs. He wanted to go back and challenge Terola, fight him to the finish, kill him, if he had to.

But as he drove in the direction of Harley Moore's studio, the brisk sea wind cooled his passions and neutralized the acid in his mind: I'm not as civilized as I like to think. There was no need to antagonize him. I handled everything wrong. Maybe I can do better with Moore.

CHAPTER 4

Bertha Moore had waited more than fifteen years for a child, and when the child, a girl, was born, Bertha could not quite believe in her good fortune. She had constantly to reassure herself. At all hours of the day and night she tiptoed into the nursery to see if the baby was still there, still alive. She could not settle down to read or sew even for a minute; she seemed to be half-suspended in air like a gas-filled balloon held captive only by a length of string. At the other end of this string, fixed and stationary, was her husband, Harley.

She did not make the mistake of ignoring Harley

after the birth of the baby. She was, in fact, extremely kind to him, but it was a planned and unemotional kindness; at the back of her mind there was always the thought that she must take deliberate pains to keep Harley contented because the baby would be healthier and better adjusted if it had a happy home and a good father.

What spare time Bertha had was spent in conversations with friends and relatives about the perfections of her child, or in frantic calls to the pediatrician when it regurgitated its food or to Harley when it cried without apparent reason. During nearly twenty years of marriage Bertha had learned not to disturb Harley at his studio. She unlearned this in a single day, easily, and without the slightest compunction. These calls were "for the baby's sake," and as such were beyond reproach and above criticism. The baby flourished, unaware of its demands on its parents. Bertha called her Angie, which was short for Angel and had no connection with her registered name, Stephanie Caroline Moore.

At 4 o'clock Angie was in no mood for her bottle. Bertha was waltzing her back and forth across the living room when the telephone rang. She shifted the baby gently from her left arm to her right and picked up the receiver.

"Hello?"

"Hello. Is that Mrs. Moore?"

"Yes."

"You don't know me, but I'm a friend of your husband's."

"Really?" Bertha said, in a lively manner, though she was hardly paying any attention. The baby's hair felt so soft against her neck and its warm skin smelled of flowers and sunshine.

"I'm Evelyn Merrick. Perhaps your husband has mentioned me?"

"He may have." With considerable effort the baby turned her head to listen to the conversation, and she made such a droll face that Bertha laughed out loud.

"Are you alone, Mrs. Moore?"

"I'm *never* alone. We have a new baby, you know."

There was a pause. "Of course I knew."

"She was just four months old yesterday."

"They're so sweet at that age."

"Aren't they, though. But Angie's more like six months than four, even the doctor says so." This was practically true. The doctor had, after considerable prompting from Bertha, agreed that Angie was "quite advanced," and was "developing nicely."

"That's such a cute name, Angie."

"It's only a nickname, really." What a nice voice the woman had, Bertha thought, and how interested she was in the baby. "Speaking of names, I'm afraid I didn't catch yours."

"Evelyn Merrick. Miss Merrick."

"It does sound familiar. I'm almost sure Harley's mentioned you. Most of the time I'm so busy with the baby I don't hear what people are saying. . . . Stop that, Angie. No, no, mustn't touch. . . . She's trying to pull out the telephone cord."

"She sounds just adorable."

"Oh, she is," Bertha had admired other women's babies for so many years—telling the truth, if the baby was cute, fibbing if it wasn't—that she felt it only just that other women now had to admire hers. The nice thing was that none of them had to fib about Angie. She was perfect. There was no compliment about her so bulky, no piece of flattery so huge, that Bertha couldn't swallow with the greatest of ease and digest without the faintest rumble.

"Does the baby look like you or like Harley?"

"Oh, like me, I'm afraid," Bertha said with a proud little laugh. "Everyone thinks so."

"I'd love to see her. I'm quite—mad about babies."

"Why don't you come over?"

"When?"

"Well, this afternoon, if you like. Angie's restless, she won't go to sleep for hours." It would be fun to show the baby off to one of Harley's friends, for a change. Harley was very modest about Angie and hardly ever brought anyone to see her. "Harley won't be home until six. We can have some tea and a chat, and I'll show you Angie's baby book. Are you an artist, by any chance, Miss Merrick?"

"In a way."

"I just wondered. Harley says the baby's too young to be painted, but I—well, never mind. You will see for yourself. You know our address?"

"Yes. It will be a pleasure meeting you, Mrs. Moore."

They said good-bye and Bertha hung up, feeling a pleasant glow of anticipation and maternal pride.

She was not, by nature or experience, a suspicious woman—Harley had dozens of friends of both sexes—and it didn't strike her as odd that Evelyn Merrick hadn't explained the purpose of her call.

"A nice lady," she told Angie, "is coming to admire you and I want you to be utterly captivating."

Angie chewed her fingers.

When the baby's diaper and dress had been changed and her half-inch of hair carefully brushed, Bertha went back to the phone to call Harley.

Harley himself answered, sounding sharp and distrustful the way he always did over the telephone, as if he expected to be bored or bamboozled.

"Har? It's just me."

"Oh. Anything wrong with the baby?"

"Not a thing. She's bright as a dollar."

"Look, Bertha, I'm awfully tied up right now. There's a man here who . . ."

"Well, I won't keep you, dear. I just wanted to tell you not to hurry home, I'm having company for tea. A Miss Merrick is coming over to see the baby."

"Who?"

"A friend of yours. Evelyn Merrick."

"She's coming there?"

"Why, yes. What's the matter, Har? You sound so . . ."

"When is she coming?"

"Well, I don't know. It was kind of indefinite."

"Listen to me carefully, Bertha. Lock the doors and stay in the house until I get home."

"I don't under—"

"Do as I say. We'll be there in fifteen minutes."

"What do you mean, we?"

"There's a man in my studio right now looking for that woman. He says she's crazy."

"But she sounded so sweet—and she was so interested in Angie and wanted to see . . ."

But Harley had hung up.

She stood, wide-eyed and pale, hugging the baby to her breasts. Angie, sensing the sudden tension, and resenting the too tight and desperate embrace, began to cry.

"Be a good girl now, Angie," Bertha said, sounding very calm. "There is nothing the matter, nothing to be afraid of."

But the calm voice did not reassure the baby; she heard the quickened heartbeat, she felt her mother's trembling muscles, and she smelled fear.

"We will simply lock the doors and wait for daddy. There's nothing to cry about. My goodness, what will the neighbors think, such a little girl making so much noise. . . ."

Carrying the howling child, Bertha locked the three outside doors and pulled the heavy drapes across the bay window in the living room. Then she sat down in the rocking chair that Harley had bought her because she'd said no one could raise a baby without one. The darkened room and the gentle rocking motion quieted the child.

"That's a sweet girl. You settle down now and go to sleep. My goodness, we mustn't get excited about a little thing like a crazy . . ."

The door chimes pealed.

Without even glancing toward the door, Bertha carried the sleeping child to the nursery and laid her in the crib and covered her with a blanket. Then she walked slowly back to the front hall as the chimes pealed again.

She stood, waiting and listening, her face like stone. There were no sounds of cars passing or children playing or women hurrying home from the super market. It was as if everyone, forewarned of danger, had moved to another part of town.

"Mrs. Moore?" The voice came, soft but persistent, through the crack of the oak door. "Let me in."

Bertha pressed the back of her hand tight against her mouth as if afraid words might come out without her volition.

"I hurried right over. I'm dying to see the baby. Let me in. . . . I know you're there, Mrs. Moore. What's the matter? Are you afraid of me? I wouldn't harm anyone. I only want to see Harley's baby. . . . Harley and I may have a baby, too."

The words seeped through the crack of the door like drops of poison that could kill on contact.

"Does that shock you, Mrs. Moore? You don't know much of what goes on in that studio of his, do you? What do you think happens after I pose naked?"

Make her stop, Bertha prayed silently. She's lying. She's crazy. Harley would never—he's not like that—he told me they were all like pieces of wood to him. . . .

"Oh, don't think I'm the only one. I'm just the latest. After the posing it comes so natural, so inevitable. Have you been fooled all these years? Haven't you wondered, in the back of your mind?

Aren't you wondering now? I should lend you my crystal ball. Oh, the things you'd see!"

And she began to describe them, slowly and carefully, as if she were instructing a child, and Bertha listened like a child, not understanding some of the ugly words she used but hypnotized by their implications of evil. She couldn't move, couldn't get out of range of the poison. Drop by drop it burned into her heart and etched nightmares on her mind.

Then, quite suddenly, from the corner, came the quick, tinkling song of a Good Humor man. "My Bonnie lies over the ocean. . . . Oh, bring back my Bonnie to me." The song ended and began again, but in the interval Bertha heard the tap of heels on concrete. Moving lifelessly, like a dummy on hinges, she walked into the living room and parted the heavy drapes on the bay window.

A woman was running down the street, her dark hair lashing furiously in the wind, her coat flapping around her skinny legs. She turned the corner, still running, heading south.

Bertha went back to the nursery. Angie was sleeping on her side with her thumb in her mouth.

Bertha stood by the crib and looked down at the baby, numbly, wondering what kind of man its father was.

"Bertha. Are you all right, dear?"

"Of course."

"We got here as soon as we could. This is Mr. Blackshear. My wife, Bertha."

"How do you do." She shook hands with Blackshear. "Would you like a drink?"

"Thanks. I would," Blackshear said.

"I will, too. I was going to have tea, but . . ." I was going to have company for tea. A nice lady was coming to admire the baby. I dressed Angie up and brushed her hair. I was feeling happy, I remember. That was a long time ago.

"Bertha, you're sure you're feeling all right?"

"Yes," she said politely. How odd Harley looked, with his crew cut and his sunburn and his horn-rimmed glasses. Not like a painter at all. Perhaps that was because he didn't do much painting any more—other things went on in his studio that were more important. . . .

Harley mixed her a bourbon highball. It tasted weak and sour, and after the first sip she just held the glass to her lips and looked over the rim of it at Blackshear. Quiet, dignified, respectable. But you couldn't tell. If you couldn't tell about Harley, you couldn't tell about anyone in the whole world.

Her hand shook, and some of the highball spilled down the front of her dress. She knew both the men had seen the little accident. They were staring at her in a puzzled way, as if they realized that something was wrong and were too diffident or polite to ask what.

"She was here," Bertha said. "She asked me to let her in, and when I wouldn't, she talked at me through the crack of the door. I didn't answer, or make any noise, but somehow she knew I was there, listening." She glanced quickly at Harley and away again. "I can't tell you what she said, in front of a stranger."

"Why not?"

"It was about you, your relations with her."

"I had no relations with her except one day last week when she came to the studio for a job and I turned her down."

"She said she was one of your—models."

"Go on," Harley said grimly. "What else?"

"She said you and she—she used terrible words —I couldn't repeat them to anyone. . . ."

The blood had drained from Harley's sunburned face, leaving it gray-tan and lifeless, like sandstone. "She implied that I had sexual relations with her?"

"*Implied.*" Bertha began to laugh. "*Implied.* That's funny, it really is. If you could have heard her . . ."

"You listened to her, Bertha?"

"Yes."

"Why?"

"I don't know. I didn't want to, I hated it, but I listened."

"Did you believe what she said?"

"No."

He accepted the faint and unconvincing denial without pressing her further. He even tried to give her a reassuring smile, but he looked sick and exhausted as he turned to Blackshear. "Is this the kind of mischief the Merrick woman goes in for?"

"It's a little more than mischief, I'm afraid."

"Well, she may be insane, but she seems to know a lot about human frailties."

"She does." Blackshear thought of the things Evelyn Merrick had said to Miss Clarvoe. She had used Miss Clarvoe's own special set of fears as she had used Mrs. Moore's, and to a lesser extent, Lydia Hudson's, not creating new fears but working on ones that were already there. In each case she had taken a different approach, but the results were the same, uncertainty, anxiety, dread. Miss Hudson had a strong enough personality to settle her own problems; Helen Clarvoe's, perhaps, would never be settled; but Mrs. Moore had a need for, and the ability to accept, help.

Blackshear said, "Evelyn Merrick gets her satisfactions out of other people's pain, Mrs. Moore. Today it was yours. But there have been others."

"I didn't—know that."

"It's true. There is absolutely no limit to what she would say to cause trouble, and perhaps in your case she had an extra motive. Mr. Moore tells me that he was busy at the time she came to the studio and he gave her a quick brush-off."

Bertha smiled, very faintly. "Harley's quite good at that."

"The Merrick woman may have wanted to pay him back. Little episodes like that, which the ordinary person would pass off easily and forget about, often become terribly exaggerated in the mind of an unbalanced woman."

"Of course, I didn't believe her for a minute," Bertha said, in a very firm, reasonable voice. "After all, Harley and I have been happily married for nearly twenty years. . . . I suppose Harley's told you about our little girl?"

"He did."

"Would you like to see her?"

"I'd like it very much."

"Let me get her," Harley said, but Bertha had already risen.

"I'll get her," she said, smiling. "I have something to tell her."

Angie was still asleep. She woke up, at Bertha's touch, and made a squeak of protest that turned into a yawn.

Bertha spoke softly into her tiny ear. "Your father is a good man. We mustn't either of us forget that. He is a *good man.*"

She carried the child into the living room, walking fast, as if she could get away from the whispers that echoed against the walls of her memory: *You don't know much of what goes on in that studio. . . . Have you been fooled all these years? . . . Oh, the things you'd see in my crystal ball. . . .*

Bertha listened.

CHAPTER 5

"Helen? Is that you, Helen dear?"

"Yes."

"This is mother."

"Yes."

"I must say you don't seem very happy to hear from me."

"I'm trying." Helen thought, she sounds the same as ever, like a whining child.

"Please speak *up,* dear. If there's one thing I can't bear it's telephone mumblers. Helen? Are you there?"

"I'm here."

"That's better. Well, the reason I wanted to speak to you, I just had a very mysterious phone call from Mr. Blackshear. You remember, that broker friend of your father's whose wife died of cancer?"

"I remember."

"Well, suddenly out of a blue sky he called and asked if he could come and see me tonight. You don't suppose it has anything to do with *money?*"

"In what way?"

"Perhaps he's discovered some misplaced stocks or bonds that belonged to your father."

"I hardly think so."

"But it's possible, isn't it?"

"Yes, I suppose."

"Wouldn't it be a lovely surprise, say just a few shares of AT&T stuck away in a drawer and forgotten. Wouldn't that be *fun?*"

"Yes." She didn't bother pointing out that her father had never bought any shares of AT&T, and if he had, they wouldn't be stuck in a drawer and forgotten. Let Verna find it out for herself; she had a whole closetful of punctured dreams, but there was always room for one more.

The expectation of money, however remote, put a bright and girlish lilt into Verna's voice. "I haven't seen you for ages, Helen."

"I realize that."

"How have you been?"

"Fine, thank you."

"Are you eating properly?"

It was an impossible question to answer, since Verna's ideas of proper eating varied week by week, depending on which new diet attracted her attention. She dieted, variously, to grow slim, to gain weight, to correct low blood sugar, to improve her complexion, to prevent allergies, and to increase the flow of liver bile. The purpose of the diet didn't matter. The practice was what counted. It gave her something to talk about, it made her more interesting and unusual. While her liver bile continued at the same old rate, Verna flitted from one diet to another, making other women who could and did eat anything look like clods.

"*Do* speak *up,* Helen."

"I didn't say anything."

"Oh. Well. The fact is, Dougie and I are having lunch tomorrow at the Vine Street Derby. It's so close to where you are that I thought you might like to join us. Would you?"

"I'm afraid not. Thanks just the same."

"But it's quite a special occasion. In the first place, it's Dougie's birthday, he'll be twenty-six. *Tempus fugit,* doesn't it? And in the second place, someone else will be there whom I'd like you to meet, Dougie's art teacher, a Mr. Terola. I'm told he's a terribly fascinating man."

"I didn't know that Douglas was interested in painting."

"Oh, not painting. Photography. Dougie says there's a big future in photography, and Mr. Terola knows practically everything there is to know about it."

"Indeed."

"I do wish you'd make an effort to come, dear. We'll be at the Derby at 1 o'clock sharp."

"I'll try to make it." She knew why her mother was anxious for her to be there. She expected her to bring a check for Douglas as a birthday present.

"Are you still there, Helen?"

"Yes."

"These long silences make me nervous, they really do. I never know what you're *thinking*."

Helen smiled grimly into the telephone. "You might ask me some time."

"I'm afraid you'd answer," Verna said with a sharp little laugh. "It's all set, then? We'll see you tomorrow at one?"

"I won't promise."

"My treat, of course. And listen, Helen dear. *Do* wear a little lipstick, won't you? And don't forget it's Dougie's birthday. I'm sure he'd appreciate some little remembrance."

"I'm sure he would."

"Until tomorrow, then."

"Good-bye."

Helen set down the phone. It was the first time in months that she had talked to her mother, but nothing had changed. Animosity still hung between them like a two-edged sword; neither of them could use it without first getting hurt herself.

"A hundred dollars," Verna said aloud. "Or two, if we're lucky. She wouldn't miss it. And if Mr. Blackshear has found those shares of AT&T, we'll be able to keep going for a little while anyway."

Verna was down to a single car, a second mortgage and a part-time servant. She had had the telephone company take out the extra phones in her bedroom and in the patio, and she'd covered the bare spot in the dining-room carpet with a cotton mat, and hung a calendar over the cracking plaster of the kitchen wall. In brief, she had done everything possible to cut expenses and keep the household running. But the household didn't run, it shuffled along like a white elephant, and each week it got farther and farther behind.

There were occasions, usually at the beginning of the month when the bills poured in, when Verna thought it would be a good thing if Douglas went out and got a job. But most of the time she was content to have him around the house. He was good company, in his quiet way, and he did a great deal of the gardening and the heavier work, when he wasn't studying. In Verna's opinion, Douglas was a born student. He hadn't finished college because of some highly exaggerated incident in the locker room of the gym, but he had continued studying on his own and had already covered ceramics, modern poetry, the French impressionists, the growing of avocados, and the clarinet. The clarinet hurt his lip, the avocado seedlings in the back yard had withered and no one seemed interested in exhibiting his ceramics or listening to him read Dylan Thomas aloud.

Through all this Douglas remained good-natured. He didn't openly blame the public for its stupidity or the nurseryman for selling him defective avocados, he simply let it be understood that he had done his best and no one could expect more.

No one did, except Verna, and the day he'd sold his clarinet, even though she hated the shriek of it, she went up to her bedroom and wept. The sale of the clarinet wasn't like the gradual loss of interest in ceramics and poetry and all the other things. There was an absolute finality about it that hit her like a fist in the stomach. Her pain was so actual and intense that Douglas sent for the doctor. When the doctor came he seemed just as interested in Douglas as he was in Verna herself. "That boy of yours looks as if he needs a good tonic," the doctor had said.

The "boy" would be twenty-six tomorrow.

"Two hundred dollars at least," Verna said. "After all, it's his birthday and she's his sister."

She covered the canary cage for the night, checked the kitchen to see if the maid had tidied it properly before she left, and went into the den where Douglas was lying on the couch, reading. He was wearing beaded white moccasins and a terry-cloth bathrobe with the sleeves partly rolled up revealing wrists that were so slim and supple they seemed boneless. His coloring was like Helen's, dark hair and the kind of chameleon gray eyes that changed color with their surroundings. His ears were like a woman's, very close-set. In the right ear lobe he wore a circle of fine gold wire. This tiny earring was one of the things he and Verna frequently quarreled about, but Douglas would not remove it.

When he heard his mother enter the room, Douglas put down his book and got up from the couch. Verna thought, with satisfaction, *at least I've brought him up to show some respect for women.*

She said, "Go and put some clothes on, dear."

"Why?"

"I'm having company."

"Well, *I'm* not."

"Please don't argue with me, dear. I have one of my headaches coming on." Verna had a whole battalion of headaches at her disposal. They came on like a swarm of native troops; when one of them was done to death, another was always ready to rush forward and take its place. "Mr. Blackshear is coming to see us. It may be about money."

She explained about the shares of AT&T that might have got stuck in a drawer, while Douglas listened with amiable skepticism, tugging gently at his golden earring.

The gesture annoyed her. "And for heaven's sake take that thing off."

"Why?"

"I've told you before, it makes you look foolish."

"I don't agree. Different, perhaps, but not foolish."

"Why should you *want* to look different from other men?"

"Because I am, sweetheart, I am."

He reached out and touched her cheek lightly.

She drew away. "Well, it seems to me . . ."

"To you, everything seems. To me, everything is."

"I don't understand you when you talk like that. And I won't have another argument about that earring. Now take it off!"

"All right. You don't have to scream." There was a thin line of white around Douglas' mouth and the veins in his temples bulged with suppressed anger. He unfastened the earring and flung it across the room. It ricocheted off the wall onto the blonde plastic top of the spinet piano, then it rolled forward and disappeared between two of the bass keys.

Verna let out a cry of dismay. "Now look what you've done!"

"I'm sick of being ordered around."

"You've wrecked my piano. Another repair bill to pay . . ."

"It isn't wrecked."

"It is so." She ran over to the piano, almost in tears, and played a scale with her left hand. The C and D keys were not stuck but they made a little plinking sound. "You've ruined my piano."

"Nonsense. I can fix it easily."

"I don't want you to touch it. It's a job for an expert." She rose from the piano bench, her lips tight as if they'd been set in cement.

Watching her, Douglas thought, there are some women who expand with the years, and some who shrink.

Verna had shrunk. Each week she seemed to grow smaller, and when Douglas called her old girl, it wasn't a term of endearment, it was what he really thought of her. Verna was an old girl.

"I'm sorry, old girl."

"Are you?"

"You know I am."

"Will you go up and change your clothes, then?"

"All right." He shrugged as if he'd known from

the very beginning that she would get her own way and it no longer mattered because he had his own methods of making her regret her authority.

"And don't forget to put on a tie."

"Why?"

"Other men wear ties."

"Not all of them."

"I don't see why you're in such a difficult mood tonight."

"I think it's the other way around, old girl. Take a pill or something."

As he passed the piano on his way out of the room, he ran his forefinger lightly along the keys, smiling to himself.

"Douglas."

He paused in the doorway, holding his bathrobe tight around his waist. "Well?"

"I met Evie and her mother downtown this afternoon."

"So?"

"Evie asked after you. She was really very pleasant considering what happened, the annulment and everything."

"I will be equally pleasant to her, if and when."

"She's such a lovely girl. Everyone said you made a very attractive couple."

"Let's not dredge that up."

"I don't suppose there's any chance you might

want to see her again? She didn't ask me that, of course, but I could sense she was still interested."

"You need a new crystal ball, old girl."

When he had gone, she began to circle the room, turning on the lamps and straightening the odd-shaped ceramic pieces on the mantel which had been Douglas' passing contribution to the art. Verna didn't understand what these pieces represented any more than she understood Douglas' poetry or his music. It was as if he moved through life in a speeding automobile, now and then tossing out of the windows blobs of clay and notes in music and half-lines of poetry that he had whipped up while stopping for the red lights. Nothing was ever finished before the lights changed, and what was tossed out of the windows was always distorted by the speed of the car and the rush of the wind.

Verna Clarvoe greeted Blackshear with an effusiveness he didn't expect, desire or understand. She had always in the past made it obvious that she considered him a dull man, yet here she was, coming out to the car to meet him, offering him both her hands and telling him how simply marvelous it was to see him again and how well he looked, not a day, not a minute, older.

"You haven't changed a bit. Confess now, you can't say the same about me!"

"I assure you I can."

She blushed with pleasure, misinterpreting his words as a compliment. "What a charming fibber you are, Mr. Blackshear. But then, you always were. Come, let's talk in the den. Since Harrison died we practically never use the drawing room. It's so big Dougie and I just rattle around in it. Helen no longer lives at home."

"Yes, I know that. In fact, that's one of the reasons I'm here."

"You've come about *Helen?*"

"Yes."

"Well," she said with a sharp little laugh. "Well. This is a surprise. I thought perhaps you were coming to see me about money."

"I'm sorry if I gave you that impression."

"It wasn't an impression, Mr. Blackshear. It was a *hope*. Very silly of me." She turned her face away. "Well, come along, we'll have a drink."

He followed her down the dimly lit hall to the den. A fire was spluttering in the raised fieldstone firepit and the room was like a kiln. In spite of the heat Verna Clarvoe looked pale and cold, a starved sparrow preserved in ice.

"Please sit down, Mr. Blackshear."

"Thank you."

She mixed two highballs, talking nervously as she worked. "Harrison always did this when he was alive. It's funny what odd times you miss people, isn't it? But you know all about that. . . . That's some of Dougie's work on the mantel. It's considered very unusual. Do you know anything about art?"

"Nothing at all," Blackshear said cheerfully.

"That's too bad. I was going to ask your opinion. Oh well, it doesn't matter now, Dougie's taken up something new. Photography. He goes into Hollywood to classes every day. Photography isn't just taking pictures, you know."

This was news to Blackshear but he said, "Tell me more."

"Well, you have to study composition and lighting and filters and a lot of things like that. Dougie's crazy about it. He's a born student."

She crossed the room, carrying the drinks, and sat down beside Blackshear on the cocoa rattan couch.

"What shall we drink to, Mr. Blackshear?"

"It doesn't matter."

"All right. We'll drink to all the millions of things in this world that don't matter. To them!"

Blackshear sipped his drink uneasily, realizing that he had never actually known Verna Clarvoe. In the past he had seen her in character, playing the role she thought was expected of her, the pretty and frivolous wife of a man who could afford her.

She was still onstage, but she'd forgotten her lines, and the props and backdrop had been removed and the audience had long since departed.

She said abruptly, "Don't stare at me."

"Was I? Sorry."

"I know I've changed. It's been a terrible year. If Harrison only knew . . . Do you believe that people who have passed on can look down from heaven and see what's happening on earth?"

"That wouldn't be my idea of heaven," Blackshear said dryly.

"Nor mine. But in a way I'd like Harrison to *know*. I mean, he's out of it, he's fine, he has no problems. *I'm* the one that's left. I'm—what's that legal term? Relict? That's what I am. A relict." She gulped the rest of her drink, making little sucking noises like a thirsty child. "This must be very boring for you."

"Not at all."

"Oh, you're always so *polite*. Don't you ever get sick of being polite?"

"I do, indeed."

"Why don't you get *im*polite then? Go on. I dare you. Get *im*polite, why don't you?"

"Very well," Blackshear said calmly. "You can't hold your liquor, Mrs. Clarvoe. Lay off, will you please?"

"Please. *Please*, yet. You just can't help yourself, you're a gentleman. A born gentleman. Dougie's a born student. He's learning photography. Did I tell you that?"

"Tell me again, if you like."

"Mr. Terola is his teacher. He's a very interesting man. Not a born gentleman, like you, but very interesting. You can't be both. Tragic, isn't it. Why don't you be impolite again? Go on. I can't hold my liquor. What else?"

"I came here to talk about Helen, Mrs. Clarvoe, not about you."

Blotches of color appeared on her cheekbones. "That's impolite enough. All right. Go ahead. Talk about Helen."

"As you may know, for the past year I've been handling her investments."

"I didn't know. Helen doesn't confide in me, least of all about money."

"Yesterday she asked me to serve in another capacity, as an investigator. A woman in town has been making threatening and obscene telephone calls; Helen is one of her victims. From what I've learned about this woman today, I believe she's dangerous."

"What do you expect me to do about it? Helen's old enough to take care of herself. Besides, what are the police for?"

"I've been to the police. The sergeant I talked to told me they get a dozen similar complaints every day in his precinct alone."

The effects of the drink were beginning to wear off. Verna's hands moved nervously in her lap and a little tic tugged at her left eyelid. "Well, I don't see how *I* can help."

"It might be a good idea if you invited her to come and stay here with you for a while."

"Here? In my house?"

"I'm aware that you're not on very friendly terms but . . ."

"There are no buts, Mr. Blackshear. None. When Helen left this house I asked her never to come back. She said unforgivable things, about Dougie, about me. Unforgivable. She must be out of her mind to think she can come back here."

"She doesn't know anything about the idea; it was entirely my own."

"I ought to have guessed that. Helen wouldn't ask a favor of me if she were dying."

"It isn't easy for some people to ask favors. Helen is shy and insecure and frightened."

"Frightened? With all that money?" She laughed. "If I had all that money I wouldn't be scared of the devil himself."

"Don't bet on that."

With a defiant toss of her head, she crossed the

room and began mixing herself another drink. As was the case with the first drink, she began reacting before she'd even uncorked the bottle.

"Mrs. Clarvoe, do you think it's wise to . . ."

"No, it's not wise. I'm a very stupid and ignorant woman. So I'm told."

"Who told you?"

"Oh, a lot of people, Harrison, Dougie, Helen, lots of people. It's a funny thing being told you're stupid and never being told how to get unstupid." She raised her glass. "Here's to all us birdbrains."

"Mrs. Clarvoe, do you do this every night?"

"Do what?"

"Drink like this."

"I haven't had a drink for months. As you said, I can't take the stuff. And I don't usually try. But tonight's different. Tonight's an end of something."

She held the glass in both hands, rotating it as she talked so that the clink of ice cubes punctuated her words.

"You think of an end as being definite, being caused by something important or calamitous. It's not like that at all. For me tonight is final, but nothing special happened, just a lot of little things. Some bills came in, the maid was rude about waiting for her salary, I met Evie on the street, the girl Dougie married, Dougie put on his earring and I made him take it off and he threw it and . . . You see? Just little things." She stared into the glass, watching the bubbles rise to the surface and burst. "Evie looked so sweet and pretty. I thought what lovely children they might have had. My grandchildren. I don't mind getting old but I'd like to have something to show for it, like grandchildren. Mr. Black-shear . . ."

"Yes?"

"Do you think there's something the matter with Douglas?"

A trickle of sweat oozed down the side of Black-shear's face, leaving a bright moist trail like a slug. "I'm afraid I can't answer that."

"No. No, of course not," she said quietly. "I shouldn't have asked. You don't know him, really. He's a—very sweet boy. He has many fine qualities."

"I'm sure he has."

"And he's extremely talented, everyone says that. Harrison was so strict with him, I tried to make it up to Dougie on the side, I encouraged him to express himself." She put the half-empty glass on the mantel and leaned closer to the fire, her bony little hands stretched out until they were almost touching the flames. "Harrison was a very cruel man sometimes. Does that surprise you?"

"Not much. Most of us are cruel on occasion."

"Not the way Harrison was. He used to . . . But

it doesn't matter now. I can tell I'm depressing you." She turned from the fire, making an obvious effort to control her emotions. "You've listened to my troubles, now you may tell me yours, if you like."

"They aren't very interesting."

"All troubles are interesting. Perhaps that's why we have them, to keep ourselves from being bored to death. Go on, tell me yours."

"Sorry, there isn't time, Mrs. Clarvoe."

"Don't leave yet. You haven't seen Dougie. He's upstairs getting dressed. Tomorrow's his birthday. We're having a little party at the Brown Derby."

While the maid waits for her salary, Blackshear thought grimly. "Wish Douglas a happy birthday for me."

"I will."

"There's just one more thing, Mrs. Clarvoe. Do you know a young woman named Evelyn Merrick?"

She looked surprised. "Well, of course."

"Of course?"

"She's Dougie's wife. She was, I mean. The marriage was annulled and she took back her maiden name."

"She lives here in town?"

"In Westwood. With her mother."

"I see." It was as simple as that. There'd been no need to ask Miss Hudson or Terola or Harley Moore. Evelyn Merrick wasn't a waif or a stranger. She had been Douglas Clarvoe's wife, Helen Clarvoe's sister-in-law. "Did Helen know the girl?"

"Know her? Why, that's how Douglas first met her. Evie and Helen went to a private school together years ago in Hope Ranch and Helen used to bring Evie home for week-ends. After graduation they went to different colleges and lost touch, but Evie used to come over here once in a while, mostly to see Douglas. Douglas had always adored her, she was such a lively, affectionate girl. She used to tease the life out of him but he loved it. There was never any malice in her teasing."

There is now, Blackshear thought. "Tell me about the wedding."

"Well, it was a very quiet one, being so soon after Harrison's death. Just the family and a few friends."

"Was Helen there?"

"Helen," she said stiffly, "had already moved out. She was invited, of course, and she sent a lovely gift."

"But she didn't come?"

"No. She was ill."

"How ill?"

"Really, Mr. Blackshear, I don't know how ill. Nor did I care. I didn't want her to come anyway. She might have ruined the wedding with that gloomy face of hers."

Blackshear smiled at the irony. Helen might have ruined the wedding, but Verna had ruined the marriage.

"Besides," Verna said, "she and Evie weren't best friends any more, they hardly ever saw each other. They had nothing much in common, even when they were at school together. Evie was quite a bit younger, and the very opposite in temperament, full of fun and laughter."

"You saw her this afternoon."

"Yes."

"Is she still full of fun and laughter?"

"Not so much any more. The breakup of the marriage was hard on her. Hard on all of us. I wanted grandchildren."

The second drink had brought color to her face and made her eyes look like blue glass beads in a doll's head.

"I wanted grandchildren. I have nothing to show for my life. Nothing."

"You have Helen. I think perhaps the two of you have reached the stage where you need each other."

"We won't discuss that again."

"Very well."

"I don't want any advice. I hate advice. I don't need it."

"What do you need, then?"

"Money. Just money."

"Money hasn't helped you much in the past. And it's not helping Helen much now. She's in the position of being able to indulge her neurosis instead of trying to do something about it."

"Why tell me?"

"I think you're the logical person to tell, since you're her mother."

"I don't feel like her mother. I never did, even when she was a baby. The ugliest baby you ever saw, I couldn't believe it belonged to me. I felt cheated."

"You'll always be cheated, Mrs. Clarvoe, if you put your value on the wrong things."

She raised her clenched right fist and took a step forward as if she meant to attack him.

Blackshear rose to meet her. "You asked me to be impolite."

"I'm asking you now to get out and leave me alone."

"All right, I'll go. Sorry if I've disturbed you."

Her hands dropped suddenly and she turned away with a sigh. "I'm the one who should apologize. I've had—it's been a bad day."

"Good night, Mrs. Clarvoe."

"Good night. And when you see Helen, tell her —tell her hello for me."

"I'll do that."

"Good night."

As soon as he had gone, she went upstairs to Douglas' room, leaning heavily on the bannister for support. I must be firm, she thought. We must reach some decision.

The door of his bedroom was open.

"Dougie, there are some things we should . . . Dougie?"

He had changed his clothes as she had ordered him to—the terry-cloth robe and the beaded moccasins he'd been wearing were on the floor beside the bed—but once again he'd made her regret the order. Instead of coming down to the den to meet Blackshear, he had left the house.

She said, "Dougie," again, but without hope. She knew he was gone, she could even visualize the scene. Douglas coming downstairs, pausing at the den door, listening, hearing his name: *Do you think there's something the matter with Douglas, Mr. Blackshear?*

She turned and moved stiffly toward the staircase. As she walked through the empty house she had a feeling that it would always be empty from now on, that the day had held a finality for Douglas as well as for herself, and he had fled the knowledge of it.

Pressing her fists against her mouth, she thought, I mustn't get silly and hysterical. Of course Dougie

will be back. He's gone out to get a pack of ciga-
rettes. Or for a walk. It's a lovely evening. He likes
to walk at night and name the stars.

The telephone in the hall began to ring. She was
so sure that it was Douglas calling that she spoke
his name as soon as she picked up the receiver.

"Douglas. Where are . . . ?"

"Is that the Clarvoe residence?"

The voice was so muffled and low that Verna
thought it was Douglas playing one of his tricks,
talking through a handkerchief to disguise his iden-
tity. "Where on earth did you disappear to? Mr.
Blackshear was . . ."

"This isn't Douglas, Mrs. Clarvoe. It's me. Evie."

"Evie. What a coincidence, I was just talking
about you."

"To whom?"

"A friend of mine, Mr. Blackshear."

"Did you say nice things?"

"Of course I did." She hesitated. "I said hello to
Douglas for you. He was very pleased."

"Was he?"

"I—I know he'd love to see you."

"Would he?"

"He said, why don't you come over some time,
we'll talk about old times."

"I don't want to talk about old times."

"You sound so funny, Evie. Is anything wrong?"

"Nothing. I only called to tell you something."

"What about?"

"Douglas. I know you're worried about him. You don't know what's the matter with him. I'd like to help you, Mrs. Clarvoe. You were always kind to me, now I will repay you."

She began to explain in detail what was the matter with Douglas and some of the things that went on in the rear of Mr. Terola's studio.

Long before she had finished, Verna Clarvoe slumped forward on the floor.

CHAPTER 6

It was nine-thirty.

The woman had been in the telephone booth for half an hour and Harry Wallaby was still waiting to call his wife in Encino and tell her the old Buick had broken down and he was going to spend the night with his brother-in-law.

"You'd think the dame's tongue'd drop off," Wallaby said over his third beer.

The bartender, a middle-aged Italian sporting a bow tie in Princeton colors, shook his head knowingly. "Not hers. The more exercise it gets, the stronger it gets. Phoneitis, that's what she has, phoneitis."

"Never heard of it before."

"It's like a disease, see. You gotta phone people. With her it's bad."

"Who is she?"

"Just a dame who comes in once in a while. Everytime it's the same routine. A couple of drinks and it hits her, wham. She gets a buck's worth of dimes and parks herself in the phone booth, and there she sits, yackity, yackity, yackity. I've often wondered what in hell she talks about."

"Why don't you find out?"

"You mean go over and listen?"

"Sure."

"It wouldn't look right, me being the owner and proprietor," the bartender said virtuously.

"The same don't go for me. Is there a law says a guy can't stand beside a telephone booth, innocent-like?"

"It's a free country."

"Damn right it's a free country."

With an elaborate pretence of casualness, Wallaby slid off the bar stool, walked toward the front entrance as if he intended to leave, and then crept up on the telephone booth from the left side. He listened a moment, his hand cupping his ear, and returned to the bar, grinning a little sheepishly.

The bartender raised his eyebrows in silent inquiry.

"She's talking about some guy called Douglas," Wallaby said.

"What about him?"

"I don't know."

"Didn't you hear anything?"

Wallaby flushed. "I must of heard wrong. I mean, I must of. Jeez, I never heard nobody talk like that before."

"Well, for Pete's sake, tell me."

"I need another drink first."

At a quarter to ten Evelyn Merrick stepped out of the telephone booth, stretched her left arm to relieve the cramp and smoothed her skirt down over her hips. Usually, after making a series of telephone calls, she felt a certain relief and relaxation, but tonight she was still excited. The blood drummed double-time in her ears and behind her eyes, and she lurched a little as she made her way back to the bar. Her old-fashioned was untouched on the counter. She didn't pick it up, she just sat down, staring at it suspiciously, as if she thought the bartender had added something to it in her absence.

"O.K., Wallaby," the bartender said loudly and pointedly, "you can phone your wife now."

Evelyn caught his meaning at once and looked up,

a flush spreading across her cheekbones. "Did I use the telephone too long?"

"Just nearly an hour, that's all."

"It's a public phone."

"Sure, it's a public phone, meaning it's for the public, for everybody. Someone like you ties it up and the rest don't get a chance. If this was the first time, I wouldn't beef."

"Do you talk to all your customers like this?"

"I own the joint. I talk how I please. People that don't like it don't gotta come back. This includes anybody."

"I see." She stood up. "Is that your liquor license beside the cash register?"

"Sure, it's my license. Paid for and up to date."

"Your name's Florian Vicente?"

"That's right."

"Well, good night, Mr. Vicente."

Vicente's jaw dropped in astonishment at her pleasant smile and friendly tone, and he felt a little ashamed of himself for being so brusque with her. After all, she was harmless.

Outside, the first rain of the season had begun, but Evelyn Merrick didn't notice. She had more important things to think about. Mr. Vicente had been rude and must be taught a lesson in manners.

She began walking along Highland toward Hollywood Boulevard, repeated the bartender's name to imprint it on her memory. Florian Vicente. Italian. Catholic. Very likely a married man with several children. They were the easiest victims of all, the married ones with children. She thought of Bertha and Harley Moore and threw back her head and laughed out loud. The rain sprayed into her open mouth. It tasted fresh and good. It tasted better than Mr. Vicente's old-fashioneds. Mr. Vicente should serve drinks like that. *Give me a double rain, Mr. Vicente. In the morning I will phone Mrs. Vicente and tell her her husband is a pimp.*

She tripped down the slippery street, her body light and buoyant, bobbing like a cork on the convulsed seas of her emotions.

People huddling in doorways and under awnings looked at her curiously. She knew they were thinking how unusual it was to see such a gay pretty girl running alone in the rain. They didn't realize that the rain couldn't touch her, she was waterproof; and only a few of the smart ones guessed the real reason why she never got tired or out of breath. Her body ran on a new fuel, rays from the night air. Occasionally one of the smart ones tried to follow her to get her secret, to watch her refueling, but these spies were quite easy to detect and she was always able to evade them. Only in the strictest privacy did she store up her rays, breathing deeply first through one nostril and then the other, to filter out the irritants.

She turned east on the Boulevard, toward Vine Street. She had no destination in mind. Somewhere along the way there would be a small bar with a telephone.

She hurried forward across the street, not seeing the red light until a woman yelled at her from a passing car and a man behind her grabbed her by the coat and pulled her back up on the curb.

"Watch your step, sister."

She turned. The man's face was half-hidden by the collar of his trenchcoat and the pulled-down brim of a green fedora. The hat splashed water like a fountain.

"Thank you," she said. "Thank you very much."

He tipped his hat. "Welcome."

"You probably saved my life. I don't know how to . . ."

"Forget it."

The light turned green. He brushed past her and crossed the street.

The whole episode had not taken more than half a minute, but already it was expanding in her mind, its cells multiplying cancerously until there was no room for reason. The half-minute became an hour, the red light was fate, the touch of his hand on her coat was an embrace. She remembered looks that hadn't been exchanged, words that hadn't been spoken. Lover. Dear one. Beloved. Beautiful girl.

Oh, my dear one, wait for me. I'm coming. Wait. Lover. Lover dear.

Soaked to the skin, exhausted, shivering, lost, she began to run again.

People stared at her. Some of them thought she was sick, some thought she was drunk, but no one did anything. No one offered her any help.

She refueled in an alley between a hotel and a movie house. Hiding behind a row of garbage cans, she breathed deeply first through one nostril and then the other. The only witness was a scrawny gray tomcat with incurious amber eyes.

Inhale. Hold. Count four.

Exhale. Hold. Count three.

It must be done slowly and with proper care. The counting was of great importance. Four and three make seven. Everything had to make seven.

Inhale. Hold. Count four.

By the time she had finished refueling, she had completely forgotten about lover. The last thing she remembered was Florian Vicente who had called her wicked names because she had discovered his secret, that he was a pimp. What a shock it would be to his wife when she found out. But the poor woman must be enlightened, the truth must be told at all costs, the word must be spread.

Shaking her head in sympathy for poor Mrs. Vicente, Evelyn walked on down the alley and into the back door of the hotel bar. She had been here before.

She ordered a martini, which had seven letters.

A young man sitting on the next stool swung round and looked at her. "It's still raining, eh?"

"Yes," she said politely. "It doesn't matter, though."

"It matters to me. I've got to . . ."

"Not to me. I'm waterproof."

The young man began to laugh. Something about the sound of his laughter and the sight of his very white, undersized teeth reminded her of Douglas.

"I'm not joking," she said. "I *am* waterproof."

"Good for you." He winked at the bartender. "I wish I was waterproof, then I could get home. Tell us how you did it, lady."

"You don't do anything. It happens."

"Is that a fact?"

"It just happens."

"Is that a fact?"

He was still laughing. She turned away. She couldn't be bothered with such an ignorant fool who had teeth like Douglas. If he persisted, of course, if he became really rude like Mr. Vicente, she would have to get his name and teach him a lesson. Meanwhile, there was work to be done.

She paid for the martini, and without even tasting it she approached the phone booth at the rear of the room and opened the folding door.

She didn't have to look up any numbers. She forgot other things sometimes, she had spells when the city seemed foreign as the moon to her and people she knew were strangers and strangers were lovers, but she always remembered the telephone numbers. They formed the only continuous path through the tormented jungle of her mind.

She began to dial, shaking with excitement like a wild evangelist. The word must be spread. Lessons must be taught. Truth must be told.

"The Monica Hotel."

"I'd like to speak to Miss Helen Clarvoe, please."

"I'm sorry, Miss Clarvoe has had a private telephone installed in her suite."

"Could you tell me the number?"

"The number's unlisted. I don't know it myself."

"You filthy liar," Evelyn said and hung up. She couldn't stand liars. They were a bad lot.

She called Bertha Moore, but as soon as Bertha recognized her voice, she slammed down the receiver.

She called Verna Clarvoe again. The line was busy.

She called Jack Terola's studio, letting the phone

ring for a full minute in case he was busy in the back room, but there was no answer.

She called the police and told them a man had been stabbed with a scissors in the lobby of the Monica Hotel and was bleeding to death.

It was better than nothing. But it wasn't good enough. The power and excitement were rotting away inside her like burned flesh, and her mouth was lined with gray fur like the tomcat's in the alley.

The cat. It was the cat that had ruined everything, it had contaminated her because it saw her refueling. She liked animals and was very kind to them, but she had to pay the cat back and teach it a lesson, not with a phone but a scissors. Like the man in the lobby.

The man was no longer part of her imagination but part of her experience. She saw him clearly, lying in the lobby, white face, red blood. He looked a little like Douglas, a little like Terola. He was Douglas-Terola and he was dead.

She returned to the bar. One of the bartenders and the young man who had laughed at her were talking, their heads close together. When she approached they pulled apart and the bartender walked away to the other end of the bar. The young man gave her a hurried uneasy glance and then he got up and he, too, walked away toward the back exit.

Everyone was deserting her. People did not answer their phones, people walked away from her. Everyone walked away. She hated them all, but her special hate was reserved for the three Clarvoes, and, of the three, Helen in particular. Helen had turned her back on an old friend, she had walked away, first and farthest, and for this she must suffer. She couldn't hide forever behind an unlisted telephone number. There were other ways and means.

"I'll get her yet," Evelyn whispered to the walls. "I'll get her yet."

The fur in her mouth grew long and thick with hate.

CHAPTER 7

Dawn came, a misty, meager lightening of the sky. The storm had intensified during the night. A banshee wind fled screaming up and down the streets, pursued by the rush of rain.

But it was not the wind or the rain that awakened Miss Clarvoe. It was the sudden stab of memory.

"Evie," she said, the name which had meant nothing to her for a long time was as familiar as her own.

Her heart began to pound and tears welled up in her eyes, not because she remembered the girl again, but because she had ever forgotten. There was no reason to forget, no reason at all. Right from the beginning they had been the closest of friends. They exchanged clothes and secrets and food from home, giggled together after the lights were out, met between classes, invented a language of their own to baffle the interceptors of notes, and shared the same crush on the science master who was married and had four children and large romantic brown eyes. Other crushes, too, they shared, but they were all Evie's to begin with. Helen just followed along, content to have Evie take the lead and make the decisions.

We were friends, always. Nothing ever happened that I should forget her. There's no reason, no reason.

They had attended their first dance together one Hallowe'en, dressed alike, at Evie's suggestion, in gypsy costumes. Evie carried a goldfish bowl as a substitute for a crystal ball.

The dance, to which all the upper school girls had been invited, was held in the gymnasium of a private boys' school in the valley. Mr. Clarvoe drove Helen and Evelyn to the school and left them at the gym door. They were nervous and excited and full of the wildest hopes and the most abysmal fears.

"I can't go in, Evie."

"Don't be silly. They're only *boys*."

"I'm scared. I want to go home."

"We can't walk ten miles dressed like this. Come on in, be a sport."

"Promise you won't leave me?"

"I promise."

"Cross your heart."

"Listen to the music, Helen. They've got a real orchestra!"

They went inside and almost immediately they were separated.

The rest of the evening was a nightmare for Helen. She stood in a corner of the room, rigid, tongue-tied, watching Evie surrounded by boys, laughing, humming snatches of music, floating gracefully from one partner to another. She would have given her soul to be Evie, but no one offered her the chance.

She went into the lavatory and cried, her forehead pressed against the wall.

When the dance was over, her father was waiting in the car outside the gym.

He said, "Where's Evie?"

"A boy asked to take her home. She's going with him."

"She's altogether too young for that sort of thing. If she were my daughter I wouldn't allow it." He pulled away from the curb. "Did you have a good time?"

"Yes."

"Tell me about it."

"There's not much to tell. It was fun, that's all."

"That's not a very good description. Your mother and I went to considerable trouble to get you to this dance. We'd like some report on it at least."

She knew from his tone that he was angry but she didn't know what caused the anger and why it should be directed against her. "I'm sorry if I kept you waiting, daddy."

"You didn't." He'd been waiting for three-quarters of an hour but it was not her fault. He had come early deliberately, because it was her first dance and he was as uneasy about it as she was. He had sat in the car, listening to the chaos of laughter and music coming from the gym, imagining the scene inside, and Helen in the very center of it, bright and gay in her gypsy costume. When at last she came out, alone, with that stiff sullen look on her face, disappointment rose up and choked him so that he could hardly breathe.

"Did you dance with anyone?"

"Yes."

"Who?"

She didn't want to lie but she knew she had to, and she did it well. Without hesitation she described some of the boys she'd seen dancing with Evie and gave them names and invented conversations and incidents.

She talked all the way home, while her father smiled and nodded and made little comments. "That Jim sounds like a real cut-up." "Too bad the Powers boy was shorter than you." "Now, aren't you glad we made you go to dancing school?"

Later, when she kissed him good night, he gave her an affectionate little pat on the bottom.

"I'll have to watch out for you now, young lady. One of these days I'll be driven out of house and home by those little idiots hanging around."

"Good night, daddy."

"I forgot to ask about Evie. Did she have as good a time as you did?"

"I guess so. I was too busy to pay her any attention."

She went to bed, half-believing in her own lies because her father's belief was so complete.

The following day the dean of Helen's school, who had been one of the chaperones, telephoned Mr. Clarvoe. She wanted, she said, to check up on Helen and see if she was all right, she'd been so unhappy at the dance.

Nothing was said at dinner in front of Verna and Douglas, but later Mr. Clarvoe called Helen into the den and shut the door.

"Why did you lie, Helen?"

"About what?"

"The dance."

She stood, mute, scarlet with humiliation.

"Why did you lie?"

"I don't know."

"If it had been just one lie—but it was a whole string of them. I can't understand it. Why?"

She shook her head.

"Nothing of what you told me was true?"

"No, nothing," she said with a kind of bitter satisfaction, knowing he was hurt almost as much as she was. "Not a word."

"All the boys—they weren't even real?"

"I made them up."

"Helen, look at me. I want the truth. I demand it. What really happened at the dance?"

"I hid in the lavatory."

He stepped back, as if the words had struck him across the chest. "You hid—in the lavatory."

"Yes."

"Why? For God's sake, *why*?"

"I couldn't think of anything else to do."

"My God, why didn't you phone me? I'd have come and taken you home. Why didn't you let me *know*?"

"I was too—proud."

"You call that pride? Skulking in a lavatory? It's almost obscene."

"I couldn't think of anything else to do," she repeated.

"What about Evie? Was she with you?"

"No. She was dancing."

"The entire evening she was dancing and you were hiding in the lavatory?"

"Yes."

"For heaven's sake, why?"

"She was popular and I wasn't."

"Going off and hiding like that, you didn't give yourself a chance to be popular."

"I wouldn't have been anyway. I mean, I'm not pretty."

"You'll be pretty enough in time. Why your mother is one of the prettiest women in the state."

"Everyone says I take after you."

"Nonsense. You look more like your mother every day. What on earth put the idea in your head that there's anything the matter with your appearance?"

"The boys don't like me."

"That's probably because you're too standoffish. Why can't you try to be more friendly, like Evie?"

She didn't tell him what he should have known for himself—that she would have given anything in the world to be like Evie, not just at the dance, but any time, any place.

His anger, which in the beginning had boiled out like lava, was now cooling, leaving a hard crust of contempt. "You realize, of course, that I'll have to punish you for lying?"

"Yes."

"Are you sorry you lied?"

"Yes."

"There's only one true test of penitence. If you had a chance to repeat the lies, knowing you wouldn't be found out, would you do it?"

"Yes."

"Why?"

"It would have made both of us happier."

It was true and he knew it as well as she did, but he shook his head and said, "I'm disappointed in you, Helen, extremely disappointed. You may go to your room."

"All right." She lingered wanly at the door. "What about my punishment?"

"Your punishment, Helen, is being you, and having to live with yourself."

Later in the evening she heard her parents talking in their bedroom and she crept down the dark hall to listen.

"Well, heaven knows I've done everything I can, Verna said. "You can't make a silk purse out of a sow's ear."

"What about my idea of giving her a big party, inviting a bunch of boys . . ."

"What boys?"

"We must know some people who have boys about her age."

"I can think of exactly two, the Dillards and the Pattersons. I loathe Agnes Patterson, and besides, the whole idea of a party wouldn't work."

"We've got to think of something. If she goes on like this she may not even marry."

"I just don't understand you, Harrison. For years you've been treating Helen as if she were about four, and now suddenly you're thinking about her marriage."

"Are you blaming the situation on me?"

"Someone's to blame."

"But never you."

"I," Verna said righteously, "am bringing up Dougie. The girl is the father's responsibility. Besides, she takes after you. Half the time I don't even understand her. She won't speak out, let anyone know what she's thinking or how she feels about things."

"She's shy, that's all. We must find a way to get her over her shyness."

"How?"

"Well, for one thing, I think we should encourage her relationship with Evie. The girl's a good influence on Helen."

"I agree." There was a silence, and then a sigh, "What a pity we didn't have a girl like Evie."

Barefooted, shivering with cold and fear, she trudged back to her room and got into bed. But the walls and ceiling seemed to contract, to press down on her until they fitted her like a coffin. She knew then that her father had been right. This was her punishment, to be herself, and to have to live with herself forever, a living girl inside a locked coffin.

She lay awake until morning, and the emotion that was strongest in her heart was not resentment against her parents but a new and bitter hatred for Evie.

She did nothing about this hatred. It was buried with her inside the coffin and no one else knew it was there. Things went on as before, with her and Evie, or almost as before. They still shared a crush on the science master with the romantic eyes, they wrote notes in their secret language, and exchanged clothes, and food from home, and confidences. The difference was that Helen's confidences were not real. She made them up just as she'd made up the boys, and the incidents at the dance, for her father.

At the end of the spring semester, when Evie acquired a boy friend, Helen acquired two. When Evie was promised a horse as a reward for good grades, Helen was promised a car. It became as difficult for Evie to accept these lies as it was for Helen to keep on inventing them, and the two girls began to avoid each other.

There was trouble about it at home, but Helen had anticipated it and she was ready.

"Why didn't you bring Evie with you for the week-end?" her father asked.

"I invited her to come. She didn't want to."

"Why not?"

She hesitated just the right amount of time to rouse his curiosity. "I promised not to tell."

"I'm your father, you can tell me."

"No, I can't."

"Well, is it anything *we've* done?"

"Oh no. It's just—she's busy, she wanted to stay at school and study for the Latin test."

"That doesn't sound like Evie to me, staying at school when she could be here having a good time."

"Oh, she'll be having a good—I mean, she likes to study."

"You mean she's not going to be studying, isn't that it?"

"I promised not to tell."

"This sounds like the kind of thing I'd better get to the bottom of, right here and now. Where is Evie?"

"At school."

"Why?"

"I can't tell you. I made a solemn vow."

"I want an immediate and truthful answer to my question, do you hear me, Helen?"

"Yes. But . . ."

"And no but's, if's and when's, please."

"She—she has a boy friend."

"Yes? Go on."

"She doesn't want her parents to find out about him because he's a Mexican."

"A *Mexican.*"

"He works on a lemon ranch near the school. She climbs out of the window after the lights are out and meets him in the woods." She began to cry. "I didn't want to tell. You made me. You made me a liar!"

Miss Clarvoe lay in bed with her right arm across her face as if to shield herself from the onslaught of memories. The ceiling pressed down on her, the walls contracted, until they fitted her like a coffin, tight, airless, sealed forever. And locked in with her were the mementos of her life: *"Your punishment is being you and having to live with yourself." "What a pity we didn't have a girl like Evie!"*

CHAPTER 8

The house was set in the middle of a tiny walled garden on Kasmir Street in Westwood. An engraved card in a slot above the doorbell read: Mrs. Annabel Merrick, Miss Evelyn Merrick.

The house needed paint, the woman who answered Blackshear's ring did not. She looked like a farmer's wife, plump and tanned and apple-cheeked, but her clothes were city clothes, a smart black-and-white-striped suit that hinted at severely disciplinary garments underneath.

"Mr. Blackshear?"

"Yes."

"I'm Annabel Merrick." They shook hands. "Come in, won't you? I'm just making breakfast. If you haven't had yours, I can pop another egg in the pan."

"I've eaten, thank you."

"Some coffee then." She closed the front door after him and led the way through the living room into the kitchen. "I must say I was surprised by your early phone call."

"Sorry if I got you out of bed."

"Oh, you didn't. I work, you know. In the flower shop of the Roosevelt Hotel. Sure you wouldn't like an egg?"

"No, thanks."

"I've been divorced for several years, and of course alimony payments don't rise with the cost of living, so I'm glad to have a job. Somehow it's not so much like work when you're surrounded by flowers. Delphiniums are my favorite. Those blues— heavenly, just heavenly."

She brought her plate of eggs and toast to the table and sat down opposite Blackshear. She appeared completely relaxed, as if it was the most normal thing in the world to entertain strange men before 8 o'clock in the morning.

"Blackshear, that's an odd name. Do people ever get mixed up and call you Blacksheep?"

"Frequently."

"Here's your coffee. Help yourself to cream and sugar. You didn't tell me what business you were in."

"Stocks and bonds."

"Stocks and bonds? And you want to see Evelyn? Heavens, you're barking up the wrong tree. Neither of us is in a position to invest a nickel. As a matter of fact, Evelyn's out of a job right now."

"It won't hurt to talk to her."

"I guess not. As I told you on the phone, she's not here at the moment. She's spending two or three days with a friend whose husband is out of town. The friend hates to stay alone at night and Evelyn's always anxious to oblige. She's that kind of girl, she'd do anything for a friend."

Her tone was proud and maternal and Blackshear deduced from it that Mrs. Merrick was as blind about her daughter as Verna Clarvoe was about her son. He said, "May I have this other woman's name and address?"

"Certainly. It's Claire Laurence, Mrs. John Laurence, 1375 Nessler Avenue, that's near U.C.L.A. Evelyn won't be there during the day, she's looking for a job, but she'll arrive around dinnertime, I expect."

"What kind of job is she looking for? I might be able to help."

"I'm afraid stocks and bonds aren't in Evelyn's line."

"What is her line, Mrs. Merrick? Is she stage-struck? Does she want to be a model, or something like that?"

"Good heavens, no! Evelyn's a sensible and mature girl. What on earth gave you the idea she might want to be a model?"

"A lot of pretty girls do."

"Evelyn's pretty enough, but she's not vain, and she has far too many brains to enter a profession that's so temporary. Evelyn wants a future. More coffee?"

"No, thank you." But she didn't seem to hear him. She poured more coffee into his cup, and he noticed that her hand was trembling.

He said, "I hope I haven't upset you in any way, Mrs. Merrick."

"Perhaps you have. Then again, perhaps I was upset to begin with."

"Are you worried about Evelyn?"

"What else does a mother worry about, especially when there's only one child? I want Evelyn to be happy, that's all I ask for her, that she be happy and secure."

"And isn't she?"

"I thought she was, for a while. And then she

changed. Ever since her marriage she's been different." She looked across the table with a bleak little smile. "I don't know why I should tell you that, you said on the phone you don't even know Evelyn."

"I don't. I've heard of her, though, through the Clarvoes."

"The Clarvoes are friends of yours?"

"Yes."

"You know about the marriage, then?"

"Yes."

"Is that why you're here? Did Verna send you to make amends?"

"No."

"I thought perhaps—well, it doesn't matter now. It's over. Spilled milk and all that." She took her empty plate to the sink and began rinsing it under the tap. "My own marriage failed. I had high hopes for Evelyn's. What a fool I was not to *see*."

"See what, Mrs. Merrick?"

"You know what." She turned so suddenly that the plate fell out of her hands and crashed in the sink. She didn't even notice. "My daughter married a homosexual. And I let her. I let her because I didn't know it, because I was blind. I was taken in, the way Evelyn was, by his gentleness and his pretty manners and his so-called ideals. I thought what a kind and considerate husband he would make. Do you begin to see the picture Evelyn had of him?"

"Yes, clearly."

"I guess it's happened to other girls, but it wouldn't have happened to Evelyn if I hadn't been divorced, if her father had been here. He'd have known right away that there was something wrong with Douglas. As it was, we had no hint, no warning at all.

"They went to Las Vegas for their honeymoon. I had a post card from Evelyn saying she was fine and the weather was beautiful. That was all, until the doorbell rang one night a week later, and when I opened the door there was Evelyn standing on the porch with her suitcases. She didn't cry or make a fuss, she just stood there and said in a matter-of-fact way, 'I've left him. It wasn't a marriage. It was only a wedding.'

"It was a terrible shock, terrible. I kept asking her if she was sure, I told her some men were like that at first, timid and embarrassed. But she said she was sure, all right, because he had admitted it. He had apologized. Can you beat it? He apologized for marrying her! I know now how much suffering that apology cost him. I'm not blaming Douglas any more. How can I? But at the time all I cared about was Evie.

"She left her suitcases out on the porch, wouldn't

even let me bring them into the house, and the next day she took them down to the Salvation Army, her whole trousseau, wedding dress and all. When she came back around lunchtime she looked so pale and exhausted my heart turned over with pity—yes, and guilt, too. I should have known. I've been around. I was responsible."

Mrs. Merrick turned back to the sink, gathered up the bits of broken plate and tossed them into the trash can. "A plate breaks and you throw it away. A person breaks and all you can do is pick up the pieces and try to put them together the best way you can. Oh, Evelyn didn't break, exactly. She just —well, sort of lost interest in things. She'd always been an outgoing and lively girl, very quick to express her opinions or her feelings. On the night she came home she should have made a fuss, I ought to have encouraged her to talk and cry out a little of the hurt. But she was withdrawn, detached. . . ."

"Evelyn, dear, did you have dinner?"

"I think so."

"Let me heat up a little soup for you. I made some corn chowder."

"No, thank you."

"Evelyn—baby . . ."

"Please don't get emotional, Mother. We have to make plans."

"Plans?"

"I'll get an annulment, I suppose. Isn't that what
I'm entitled to when the marriage wasn't consum-
mated, as they say?"

"I think so."

"I'll see a lawyer tomorrow morning."

"There's no need for such haste. Give yourself a
chance to rest up."

"Rest up from what?" Evelyn said with a wry
smile. "No. The sooner the better. I've got to shed
that name Clarvoe. I hate it."

"Evelyn. Evelyn dear. Listen to me."

"I'm listening."

"He didn't—mistreat you?"

"You have," Evelyn said distinctly, "quite the
wrong picture. I'll give you the right one, if you
like."

"Not unless you feel like it, dear."

"I don't feel one way or the other. I just don't
want you to get the idea in your head that I was
physically abused." As she talked she rubbed the
third finger of her left hand, as if massaging away
the marks of her wedding ring. "It began on the
plane when he became sick. I thought at the time
it was airsickness, but I realize now he was sick with
fear, fear of being alone with me.

"When we arrived at the hotel, he went into the
bar while I unpacked. He stayed in the bar all night.
I waited for him, all dressed up in my flossy night-

*gown and negligee. Around 6 o'clock in the morning
two of the bellboys brought him up and poured
him out on the bed. He was snoring. He looked so
funny, yet so pathetic, too, like a little boy. As soon
as he began to show signs of waking up, I went
over and spoke to him and stroked his forehead. He
opened his eyes and saw me bending over him. And
then he let out a scream, the queerest sound I ever
heard, an animal sound. I still didn't know what the
trouble was, I thought he merely had a hangover."
Her mouth twisted with distaste and contempt.
"Well, he had a hangover, all right, but the party
had been years and years ago."*

"Oh, Evelyn. Baby . . ."

"Please don't fuss."

*"But why, why in heaven's name did he marry
you?"*

*"Because," Evelyn said dryly, "he wanted to prove
he was a man."*

Blackshear listened, pitying the woman, pitying
them all; Evelyn waiting in her flossy nightgown
for the bridegroom, Douglas sick with fear, Verna
trying desperately to hide the truth from herself.

"Yesterday," Mrs. Merrick continued, "Evelyn
met me downtown at noon to do some shopping. For
the first time since the wedding we saw Verna Clar-
voe. I was quite upset, I could think of nothing but
bitter things to say. But Evelyn was perfectly con-

trolled. She even asked about Douglas, how he was and what he was doing and so on, in the most natural way in the world."

"Verna went into that spiel of hers—Dougie was fine, he was taking lessons in photography, and doing this and doing that. It seemed to me that she was trying to start the whole business over again, trying to whip up Evelyn's interest. And then it struck me for the first time, she doesn't *know*, Verna still doesn't know, she still has hopes, doesn't she?"

"I think she has."

"Poor Verna," she said quietly. "I feel especially sorry for her today."

"Why especially?"

"It's his birthday. Today is Douglas' birthday."

CHAPTER 9

Douglas' door was locked; it was the only way she had of knowing that he had come back some time during the night, perhaps because he wanted to, perhaps because he had no place else to go.

She knocked and said, "Douglas," in a harsh heavy voice that was like a stranger's to her. "Are you awake, Douglas?"

From inside the room there came a mumbled reply and the soft thud of feet striking carpet.

"I want to talk to you, Douglas. Get dressed and come downstairs. Right away."

In the kitchen, the part-time maid, a spare elderly

woman named Mabel was sitting cross-legged at the breakfast bar, drinking a cup of coffee and reading the morning *Times*. She didn't rise when she saw Verna, who owed her back wages in civility as well as cash.

"There's muffins in the oven. Yesterday's. Heated up. You want your orange juice now?"

"I'll get it myself."

"I made a grocery list. We're out of eggs and coffee again. I need a drop of coffee now and then to steady myself and there's barely a cup left in the pot."

"All right, go and buy some. You might as well do the rest of the shopping while you're at it. We need some 100-watt bulbs and paper towels, and you'd better check the potato bin."

"You want I should do it now, before I have a bite to eat?"

"Our understanding was that you were to eat before you come here."

"We had *other* understandings too."

"You'll be paid this week. I expect a check in the mail today."

When the maid had gone, Verna took the muffins out of the oven and tested one. It was rubbery, and the blueberries inside were like squashed purple flies.

She added water to the coffee and reheated it,

and then she poured some orange juice out of a pitcher in the refrigerator. It smelled stale. The whole refrigerator smelled stale, as if Mabel had tucked odds and ends of food into forgotten corners.

Hearing the wheeze and rattle of Mabel's ancient Dodge as it moved down the driveway, Verna thought, I'll have to let her go, as soon as I can pay her. How awkward it is to have to keep her on because I can't afford to fire her.

Douglas came in as she was pouring herself a cup of coffee. He hadn't dressed, as she'd asked him to. He was wearing the terry-cloth robe and beaded moccasins he'd had on the previous night before Blackshear's visit. He looked haggard. The circles under his eyes were like bruises, and from his left temple to the corner of his mouth there ran three parallel scratches. He tried to hide the scratches with his hand, but the attempt only drew attention to them.

"What happened to your cheek?"

"I was petting a cat."

He sat down beside her, on her left, so that she would only see the uninjured side of his face. Their arms touched and the physical contact jabbed Verna like a needle. She got up, feeling a little faint, and walked over to the stove.

"I'll get you some muffins."

"I'm not hungry." He lit a cigarette.

"You shouldn't smoke before breakfast. Where did you go last night?"

"Out."

"You went out and petted a cat. A real big evening, eh?"

He shook his head wearily.

"What kind of cat was it that you petted?"

"Just an ordinary alley cat."

"Four-legged?"

"Most cats are four-legged."

"Not the one that scratched you."

"I don't know what you're getting at, I really don't." He turned his eyes on her, dove-colored, full of innocence. "What are you so angry about, Mother? I went for a walk last night, I saw this cat, I picked it up and tried to pet it and it scratched me. God help me, that's the truth."

"God help you, yes," she said. "No one else will."

"What brought on this somber mood?"

"Can't you guess?"

"Certainly I can guess."

"Go ahead, then."

"You tried to borrow money from Helen and she turned you down."

"Wrong."

"Mabel asked for her back wages."

"Wrong again."

"It has something to do with money, that's for sure."

"Not this time."

He got up and started toward the door. "I'm tired of this guessing game. I think I'll go up . . ."

"Sit down."

He stopped at the doorway. "Don't you think I'm too old to be ordered around like . . ."

"Sit down, Douglas."

"All right, all right."

"Where did you go last night?"

"Are we going to start that all over again?"

"We are."

"I went out for a walk. It was a nice night."

"It was raining."

"Not when I left. The rain started about 10 o'clock."

"And you just kept on walking?"

"Sure."

"Until you got to Mr. Terola's place?"

He stared at her across the room, unblinking, mute.

"That was your destination, wasn't it, one of the back rooms of Terola's studio?"

He still didn't speak.

"Or perhaps it wasn't Terola's, perhaps it was just anybody's back room. I hear your kind isn't particular." She heard herself saying the words but still she didn't believe them. She waited, her fists clenched against her sides, for the reactions she wanted from him: shock, anger, denial.

He said nothing.

"What goes on in that studio, Douglas? I have a right to know, I'm paying for those so-called 'photography' lessons of yours. Are you really learning anything about photography?"

He walked unsteadily back to the breakfast bar and sat down. "Yes."

"Are you behind the camera or in front of it?"

"I don't know—what you mean."

"You must know, other people do. I heard it myself last night."

"Heard what?"

"About the kind of pictures Terola takes. Not the sort of thing one would want in a family album, are they?"

"I wouldn't know."

"Who would know better than you, Douglas? You pose for them, don't you?"

He shook his head. It was the denial she'd been waiting for, praying for, but it was so fragile she couldn't touch it for fear it would break.

"Who's been talking to you?" he said.

"Someone called me last night after you went out."

"Who was it?"

"I can't tell you."

"If rumors are going around about me, I have a right to know who's passing them along."

She clutched at the straw. "Rumors? That's all they are then, Douglas? None of it's true? Not a word?"

"No."

"Oh, thank God, thank God!"

She rushed at him across the room, her arms outspread.

His face whitened and his body tensed as he braced himself for her caress. She stroked his hair, she kissed his forehead, she touched the scratches on his cheek with loving tenderness, she murmured his name, "Dougie. Dougie dear. I'm so sorry, darling."

Her arms entwined around him like snakes. He felt sick with revulsion and weak with fear. A scream for help rose in his throat and suffocated there: *God. God help me. God save me.*

"Dougie dear, I'm so sorry. You'll forgive me, won't you?"

"Yes."

"Oh, what a horrible mother I am, believing those lies. That's all they were, lies, lies."

"Please," he whispered. "You're choking me."

But the words were so muffled she didn't hear

them. She pressed her cheek against his. "I shouldn't have said those terrible things, Dougie. You're my son. I love you."

"Stop it! Stop!"

He tore himself out of her grasp and ran to the door, and a moment later she heard the wild pounding of his feet on the stairs.

She sat for a long time, stone-faced, marble-eyed, like a deaf person in a room of chatterers. Then she followed him upstairs.

He was lying spread-eagled across the bed, face down. She didn't go near him. She stood just inside the door.

"Douglas."

"Go away. Please. I'm sick."

"I know you are," she said painfully. "We must —cure you, take you to a doctor."

He rolled his head back and forth on the satin spread.

Questions rose on her tongue and died there: When did you first know? Why didn't you come and tell me? Who corrupted you?

"We'll go to a doctor," she said more firmly. "It's curable, it must be curable. They cure everything nowadays with all those wonder drugs they've got, cortisone and ACTH, things like that."

"You don't understand. You just don't *understand*."

"Try me. What is it? What don't I understand?"

"Please. Leave me alone."

"Is that what you want?"

"Yes."

"Very well," she said coldly. "I'll leave you alone. I have an errand to do anyway."

Something in her voice alerted him, and he rolled over on the bed and sat up. "What kind of errand? You're not going to see a doctor?"

"No, that's your duty."

"And what's yours?"

"Mine," she said, "is to see Terola."

"No. Don't go there."

"I must. It's my duty, as your mother."

"Don't go."

"I must confront this evil man, face to face."

"He's not an evil man," Douglas said wearily. "He's like me."

"Have you no shame, no sense of decency, defending a man like that to me, to your own mother?"

"I'm not defen—"

"Where's your self-respect, Douglas, your pride?"

He had so many things to say to her that the words became congested in his throat and he said nothing.

"I'm going to see this Terola and give him a piece of my mind. A man like that being allowed to run around loose, it's a disgrace. He's probably corrupted other young men besides you."

"He didn't corrupt me."

"What are you saying, Douglas? Of course he did. He was responsible. If it weren't for him you'd be perfectly normal. I'll see to it that he pays the . . ."

"Mother. Stop it."

There was a long silence. Their eyes met across the room and went on again, like strangers passing on a street.

"Terola," she said finally. "He wasn't the first, then."

"No."

"Who was?"

"I've forgotten."

"When did it happen?"

"It was so long ago that I can't remember."

"And all these years—all these *years* . . ."

"All these years," he repeated slowly, using the words like weapons against both her and himself.

He didn't hear her leave, but when he looked up again, she was gone and the door was closed.

He lay back on the bed, listening to the beat of rain on the roof, and the cheep-cheep of a disgruntled house wren complaining about the weather from under the eaves. Every sound was clear and sharp and final: the cracking of the eucalyptus trees as the wind increased, the barking of the collie next door, Mabel's old Dodge wheezing up the driveway, the slam of a car door, the murmur of the electric clock beside his bed.

It seemed that he had never really listened before, and now that he had learned how, each sound was personal and prophetic. He was the wren and the rain, he was the wind and the trees bending under the wind. He was split in two, the mover and the moved, the male and the female.

All these years, the clock murmured, *all these years.*

Verna tapped on the door again and came in. She was dressed to meet the weather, in a red plaid raincoat and a matching peaked cap.

She said, "Mabel's back. Keep your voice down. She has ears like a fox."

"I have nothing to say, anyway."

"Perhaps you'll think of something by the time I get back."

"You're not going to see Terola?"

"I told you I was."

"Please don't."

"I have some questions to ask him."

"Ask me instead. I'll answer. I'll tell you anything you want to know."

"Stop wheedling like that, Douglas. It annoys me." She hesitated. "Don't you see, I'm only doing my duty? I'm only doing what your father would have done if he were still alive. This man Terola, he's obviously corrupt, and yet you're trying to protect him. Why? You said you'd tell me anything. Why?"

He lay motionless on the bed, his eyes closed, his face gray. For a moment she thought he was dead, and she was neither glad nor sorry, only relieved that the problem had been solved by the simple stopping of a heart. Then his lips moved. "You want to know why?"

"Yes."

"Because I'm his wife."

"His . . . *What did you say?*"

"I'm his wife."

Her mouth opened in shock and slowly closed again. "You filthy little beast," she said quietly. "You filthy little beast."

He turned his head. She was standing by the bed watching him, her face distorted with loathing and contempt.

"Mother. Don't go. Mom!"

"Don't call me that. You're no part of me." She walked decisively to the door and opened it. "By the way, I forgot. Happy birthday."

Alone, he began to listen again to the clock and the wren and the rain and the trees; and then the sound of the Buick's engine racing in response to

Verna's anger. She's leaving, he thought. She's going to see Jack. I couldn't stop her.

He got up and went into the bathroom.

For almost a year, ever since his marriage to Evelyn, he'd been saving sleeping pills. He had nearly fifty of them now, hidden in an epsom-salts box in the medicine chest, capsules in various gay colors that belied their purpose. He swallowed five of them without any difficulty, but the sixth stuck in his throat for a few moments, and the seventh wouldn't go down at all. The gelatin coating melted in his mouth and released a dry bitter powder that choked him. He did not try an eighth.

He removed the blade from his safety razor, and standing over the washbasin he pressed the blade into the flesh that covered the veins of his left wrist. The razor was dull, the wound was hardly more than a scratch, but the sight of his blood oozing out made him dizzy with terror. He felt as if his knees were turning into water and his head was filling with air like a balloon.

He tried to scream, "Help! Mother!" but the words came out like a whimper.

As he fell forward in a faint his temple struck the projecting corner of the washbasin. The last sound Douglas heard was sharp and clear and final, the crack of bone.

At 10 o'clock, Miss Clarvoe, who had slept late, was just finishing her breakfast. When she heard the knocking on the door, she thought it was one of the busboys from the dining room coming to collect her tray and his tip.

She spoke through the crack of the door. "I haven't quite finished. Come back later, please."

"Helen, it's me. Paul Blackshear. Let me in."

She unlocked the door, puzzled by the urgency in his voice. "Is there anything the matter?"

"Your mother's been trying to reach you. The telephone company wouldn't give her your unlisted number so she called me and asked me to come over."

"To tell me she's canceled the birthday luncheon, I suppose."

"She's canceled it, yes."

"Well, she needn't worry about Douglas receiving a present from me. I sent a check out last night, he should get it today."

"He won't get it today."

"Why not?"

"Sit down, Helen."

She went over to the wing chair by the front window, but she didn't sit down. She stood behind it, moving her long thin hands nervously along its upholstered back, as if to warm them by friction.

"It's bad news, of course," she said, sounding detached. "You're not an errand boy, even mother wouldn't use you as an errand boy to tell me about a canceled luncheon."

"Douglas is dead."

Her hands paused for a moment. "How did it happen?"

"He tried to commit suicide."

"Tried? I thought you said he was dead."

"The doctor believes Douglas swallowed some sleeping capsules and cut one of his wrists, but the cause of death was a blow on the head. He struck his temple against the washbasin as he fell, probably in a faint."

She turned and looked out of the window, not to hide her grief, but to hide the grim little smile that tugged at the corners of her mouth. Poor Douglas, he could never finish anything properly, not even himself.

"I'm sorry, Helen."

"Why should you be? If he wanted to die, that was his affair."

"I meant I was sorry for you."

"Why?"

"Because you don't feel anything, do you?" He crossed the room and stood facing her. "Do you?"

"Not much."

"Do you ever feel anything? For anybody?"

"Yes."

"For whom?"

"I—I wish you would not get personal, Mr. Blackshear."

"My name is Paul."

"I really can't call you that."

"Why not?"

"I just can't, that's all."

"Very well."

"I . . . She stepped back and stood against the wall with her hands behind her back, like an embarrassed schoolgirl. "How is mother taking it?"

"I'm not really sure. When she called me on the telephone she seemed more angry than anything else."

"Angry at whom?"

"Evelyn Merrick."

"I don't understand. What had Evelyn to do with Douglas' death?"

"Your mother holds her responsible for it."

"Why?"

"Evelyn called your mother last night and gave her some information about Douglas and Jack Terola, the man who's supposedly been giving Douglas lessons in photography. I won't repeat the information. It wasn't pretty, though, I can tell you that. This morning your mother taxed Douglas with it and he admitted that some of it, at least, was true. Your mother wanted a showdown with Terola and actually started out to see him. Whether she saw him or not, I don't know for sure. She says she didn't, that she turned around and came back to the house. Meanwhile, the maid had found Douglas' body when she went to clean his room, and she called the doctor. The doctor was there when your mother arrived. She tried to get in touch with you immediately, and failing that, she called me and asked me to come over here."

"Why?"

"The telephone company . . ."

"I meant, why was she so anxious to have me informed right away? So she could be sure I'd send a nice fat wreath, as I sent a nice fat check?"

"That's uncharitable, Helen."

"Yes, I guess it is. I'm sorry. Life has taught me to be suspicious. I've learned the lesson too well."

"Perhaps you can unlearn it some day."

"Perhaps. It's harder to unlearn, though."

"I can help you, Helen."

"How?"

"By giving you something that's been too scarce in your life."

"What?"

"You can call it love."

"*Love.*" Violent pink spread up from her neck to her cheekbones. "No. No. You—you're just trying to be nice to me."

"I'm not trying," he said with a smile. "I *am* being nice to you."

"No. I don't want your love, anyone's. I can't accept it. It—embarrasses me."

"All right. Don't get excited. There's no hurry. I can wait."

"Wait? What will you wait for?"

"For you to unlearn some of those lessons you've been taught."

"What if I can't. What if I never . . ."

"You can, Helen. Just tell me you'll try. Will you?"

"Yes, I'll try," she whispered. "But I don't know where to start."

"You've already started."

She looked surprised and pleased. "I have? What did I do?"

"You remembered Evelyn Merrick."

"How do you know that?"

"You referred to her quite casually a few minutes ago as Evelyn. Do you remember her clearly now?"

"Yes."

"In her phone call to you the other night, when she said you'd always envied and been jealous of her, was she right, Helen?"

"She was right."

"That's no longer true, is it?"

"No. I don't envy her any more. She's to be pitied."

"Pitied, yes," he said, "but watched, too. She's all the more dangerous because she can appear quite rational on the surface."

"You've seen her, then."

"Not yet, I'll see her tonight. But I discussed her with your mother last night before the phone call, and early this morning I talked to Evelyn's own mother. Neither of them had the faintest suspicion that the girl is insane. She appears to have a completely split personality. On the one hand, she's the affectionate, dutiful daughter, as well as your mother's idea of a perfect daughter-in-law—and the latter would take quite a bit of doing, since your mother's not easy to please."

"I'm aware of that."

"On the other hand, the girl is so full of hatred and vengeance that she wants only to destroy people by turning them against one another. She's crafty, she hasn't had to do any of the destroying herself. She just throws in the bone and lets the dogs fight each other over it. And there's usually some meat of truth on the bone."

She thought of her mother and Douglas, and how they had fought throughout the years, not like dogs, or like boxers in a ring face to face, but like guerrillas stalking each other in a dark forest. Into this forest Evelyn had thrown a giant flare which lit up the trees and the underbrush and scorched the enemies out of their cover.

Poor Douglas. He was always a boy, he could never have grown up in a dark forest.

"I sent him a check for his birthday," she said dully. "Perhaps if I'd sent it sooner . . ."

"A check wouldn't have made any difference, Helen. The doctor found nearly fifty sleeping capsules in the medicine chest. Douglas had been planning this for a long time."

"Why does mother blame Evelyn for it, then?"

"She has to blame someone. And it can't be herself."

"No," she said, thinking, mother was trapped in the forest just as much as Douglas was. Years ago someone should have led them out, but there was no one except father and me, and father was too harsh and I was lost myself.

She covered her face with her hands and tears slid out between her fingers.

"Don't cry, Helen."

"Someone should have helped. Years ago someone should have *helped*."

"I know."

"Now it's too late, for Douglas, for mother." She raised her head and looked at him, her eyes softened by tears. "Maybe it's too late for me, too."

"Don't think that."

"Yes. I feel inside me that I've lived my life, I'm only waiting, like Douglas with his hoard of sleeping capsules. Perhaps I'll get another phone call, perhaps it will light up the underbrush and I won't be able to bear what I see."

"Stop it." He put his arms around her, but her body grew stiff as wood at his touch and her hands clenched into tight fists. He knew the time had not yet come, and perhaps never would.

He walked away to the other side of the room and sat down at the desk, watching the change come over her at his retreat, the relaxation of her muscles, the easier breathing, the leveling off of color in her face. He wondered if this was how they must remain for all time, a room's width away from each other.

"You're very—kind," she said. "Thank you, Paul."

"Forget it."

"I suppose now I must go home and stay with mother. That's what is expected of me, isn't it?"

"By her, yes."

"Then I'll get ready, if you'll excuse me."

"I'll drive you over, Helen."

"No, please don't bother. I'll call a cab. I don't want to interfere with your investigation."

"My investigation, as such, is almost finished. You asked me to find Evelyn Merrick. Well, I've found her."

"You think it's all over, then? Everything's settled?" Her voice was insistent. "You have no further work to do on the case?"

"There's work to be done but . . ."

"More than ever, in fact."

"Why more?"

"Because there's been a death," she said calmly. "Evelyn's not going to stop now. I think Douglas' death will actually spur her on, give her a sense of power."

It was what Blackshear himself feared but he hadn't wanted to alarm her by saying so. "It could be."

"Where did she get her information about Douglas?"

"From Terola himself, I guess."

"You mean they could be together in some extortion racket?"

"Perhaps Terola intended it that way, but Evelyn needs deeper satisfactions than money can give."

"But you think they were partners?"

"Yes. When I went to see Terola about her, he was pretty cagey. I got the impression he knew the girl a lot better than he admitted."

"So if there's any evidence against her, this man Terola would have it?"

"Evidence of what?"

"Anything that can be used to put her away some place. So far she's done nothing actionable. In Douglas' case she didn't even tell a lie. She can't be sued or sent to jail just for phoning mother and telling her the truth. And yet, to a certain extent, she's morally guilty of Douglas' death. You've got to stop her, Paul, before she goes on." She turned so that he couldn't see her face. "I may be next."

"Don't be silly, Helen. She can't call you, she doesn't know your number. And if she comes to the door, don't let her in."

"She'll think of some other way. I feel she's—she's waiting for me."

"Where?"

"I don't know."

"Look, if you're nervous about going over to your mother's house, let me drive you."

She shook her head. "I'd rather you went to see Terola. Tell him about Douglas, force him to talk, to give you information that can be used in court."

"That's a tall order, Helen. Even if he knows Evelyn like a book, he's not going to read it aloud to me. He'd incriminate himself."

"You can try, can't you?"

"That's about it. I can try."

He waited while she went into the bedroom to dress for the street. When she came out she was wearing a dark gray woolen coat and an old-fashioned black felt hat with a broad brim turned down over her forehead. The outfit made her look as if she'd stepped out of the previous decade.

"Helen."

"Yes?"

"Mind if I say something personal?"

"You usually do, whether I mind or not."

"You need some new clothes."

"Do I?" she said indifferently. "I never pay much attention to what I wear."

"It's time you started."

"Why?"

"Because you and I will be going places together. All kinds of places."

She smiled slightly, like a mother at the exaggerated plans of a small boy.

They took the elevator downstairs and walked through the lobby together. Mr. Horner, the desk clerk, and June Sullivan, the emaciated blonde at the switchboard, watched them with undisguised curiosity and exchanged small ugly smiles as they paused at the swinging door that led to the street.

"My car's a couple of blocks away. Sure you don't want me to drive you over to your mother's?"

"It isn't necessary."

"I'll come there later to see you, if you like."

"I'm afraid it won't be a very cheerful household. Perhaps you'd better not."

"Shall I call you a cab?"

"The doorman will."

"All right. Good-bye, then."

"Good-bye."

Outside, on the busy street, Evelyn Merrick was waiting for her.

CHAPTER 11

The wind had blown the storm out to sea and the streets, which had been fairly quiet half an hour before, now came alive, as if the end of the rain was an all-clear signal for activities to resume immediately and simultaneously. People marched briskly up and down the sidewalks like ants patrolling after a storm, but on the road traffic came almost to a standstill. Cars moved slowly, if at all, defeated by their own numbers.

It took Blackshear ten minutes to get his car out of the parking lot and another thirty to reach the

long narrow stucco building on Vine Street which
served as Terola's studio.

For the second time Blackshear read the black
stenciling on the frosted-glass window, but now the
words had more sinister implications:

PHOTOGRAPHIC WORKSHOP

JACK TEROLA, PROPRIETOR

PIN-UP MODELS · LIFE GROUPS FOR AMATEURS
AND PROFESSIONALS · RENTAL STUDIOS FOR ART GROUPS

Come in Any Time

The office was exactly as it had been the previous
afternoon except that someone had recently used
the old brick fireplace. The remains of a fire were
still smoking, and whatever had been burned had
generated enough heat to make the room uncom-
fortably hot.

The heat drew out other odors, the smell of
boiled-over coffee and of a sharp, musky perfume.
The coffee smell came from Terola's alcove, con-
cealed from view by a pair of dirty flowered-chintz
curtains. The odor of perfume came from the girl
seated behind, and almost hidden by, the old-fash-
ioned rolltop desk. She was leaning back in the
swivel chair at an awkward angle, and her eyes
were closed. She appeared to be asleep.

Blackshear recognized her as Nola Rath, the

young girl who'd been posing for one of Terola's magazine layouts the preceding day. At that time her long black hair had been wet and she'd worn no make-up. Now her hair was compressed into a roll on top of her head and she had on a layer of cosmetics so thick it was like a mask. She looked years older.

He approached the desk, diffident and a little embarrassed, feeling that he was intruding on her privacy by watching her in her sleep.

"Miss Rath?"

Slowly, as if the movement hurt her, she opened her eyes. There was no recognition in them, of Blackshear, or of anything else. She seemed dazed.

"I'm sorry if I woke you up."

"I wasn't—asleep." Her voice matched her eyes; it was flat and dull and expressionless. She held her hand to her throat as if the act of speaking, like the act of moving her eyelids, was painful to her.

"Are you feeling all right, Miss Rath?"

"All right."

"Let me get you a glass of water."

"No. No water." She shifted her weight and the chair creaked under it. "You better get out of here."

"I just came."

"That don't matter, you better go."

"I'd like to see Mr. Terola, if I may. Is he in?"

"He's not seeing anybody."

"If he's too busy right now, I'll come back later."

"He's not busy."

"Well, is he ill or something?"

"He's not ill. He's something. He's very something." She began to move her head back and forth. "I been sitting here. I don't know what to do. I been sitting. I ought to get out of here. I can't move."

"Tell me what's happened."

She didn't answer but her eyes shifted toward the alcove. Blackshear crossed the room, drew back the curtains of the alcove and stepped inside.

Terola was lying on his back on the day bed with a pair of barber's shears stuck in the base of his throat. A soiled sheet and a blood-spattered pink blanket covered the lower half of his body; the upper half was clothed in an undershirt. On a table near the foot of the day bed the hot plate was still turned on and the coffee pot had boiled dry. It looked as though Terola had got up, turned on the coffee, and then gone back to bed for a few more minutes. During those few minutes he'd had a visitor.

Whoever the visitor was, Terola had not been alarmed. There were, except for the blood, no signs of violence in the room, no evidence of a struggle. Terola's hair was not even mussed; the same thin parallel strands of gray crossed the top of his pate like railroad ties. Either Terola had known the visitor well and been taken completely by surprise, or else he'd been killed in his sleep.

The thrust of the scissors had been deep and vicious and accurate. It was a woman's weapon, a scissors, but the hand that used it had a man's strength.

In life Terola had been unprepossessing enough, in death he was monstrous. The eyes bulged like balls of glass, the fleshy mouth hung slack, the tongue, grayish pink and thick, lolled against the tobacco-stained teeth. Blackshear thought of Douglas and his youth and good looks, and he wondered what dark paths had led him to Terola.

Without touching anything, he returned to the girl in the office.

"Have you called the police?"

She blinked. "Police? No."

"Did you kill Terola?"

"No. For God's sake, no! He was my friend, he gave me a job when I was down and out, he treated me good, never slapped me around like some."

"You found him the way he is now?"

"Yes, when I came to work."

"When was that?"

"Fifteen, twenty minutes ago, I guess. Be here at noon, he said, only I always come a little early so's I can get ready."

"Was the door locked when you arrived?"

"No. Jack doesn't—didn't keep it locked unless he's—unless he was out."

"Did Terola always sleep at the office?"

"No. He and his mother and his brother have a little ranch out in the valley where they raise avocados, only Jack wasn't stuck on the place, or the company either, I guess, so he often just stayed here in town." She pressed a handkerchief to her eyes. "Oh God, I can't believe he's dead. He was going to do big things for me, he said. He said I had a great future, all I needed was some publicity. He promised he'd get me all the publicity I wanted."

Blackshear was firm. "Well, he kept his promise."

"Kept it? No, he didn't. What do you mean?"

"You'll get all the publicity you want, Miss Rath. Maybe more."

Her reaction was not what he expected. "My God, that's right. Say, there'll be newspaper photographers and everything. The works. How do I look?"

"Great."

"Gee, maybe I could even write an article for the Sunday papers about what a stinker Jack was, except to me. How's that for an angle? Here is this bum Terola, who everybody hates his guts, only he puts himself out to be kind to a down-and-out orphan girl. How does that sound?"

"Are you an orphan, Miss Rath?"

"I could be," she said with a cold little smile. "Depending on the stakes, I could be anything."

"Including a liar."

"Oh, that. Sure."

"You didn't phone the police, did you?"

She shrugged. "No. I will, though. As soon as you get out."

"Why should I get out?"

"Because you'll wreck everything for me. My future depends on this. It's gotta be done right, see?"

"I don't see."

"Well, put it this way. Suppose I didn't have so many clothes on, and suppose I run screaming into the street that I found a murdered man—get the picture?"

"Vividly."

"Then you see how you'd gum things up by being here." She stood up and leaned across the desk toward him. "I didn't kill Jack and I won't touch anything, I promise. Go away, will you, mister? I need a chance. A real chance."

"And you think this is a real chance for you?"

"It's *got* to be. I'll never get another. Now will you go? Will you *please* go, mister?"

"After you call the police."

She picked up the phone and dialed. While she

waited for an answer, she began unbuttoning her dress.

Blackshear went out to his car. He would have liked to stay behind the wheel for a few minutes to witness Nola Rath's performance, but he had a more important matter to attend to. Sometime, during the morning Verna Clarvoe had set out to see Terola. Had she, in spite of her story to the contrary, seen him, talked to him? Or had she despaired of words as a weapon and used a scissors instead? Perhaps other people had motives for killing Terola, but Verna's was fundamental, for in her, love and hate had merged and exploded like two critical masses of uranium. In the explosion, Douglas had died. Perhaps Terola was the second victim of the chain reaction.

CHAPTER 12

A red-eyed maid answered the door.

Blackshear said, "May I see Mrs. Clarvoe, please?"

"She's not seeing anybody. There's been an accident."

"Yes, I know. I have something urgent to tell Mrs. Clarvoe."

"What's more urgent than being allowed to be alone with your grief, I'd like to know?"

"What's your name?"

"Mabel."

"Mabel, I want you to tell Mrs. Clarvoe that Paul Blackshear is here on important business."

"All right, but I warn you, she's been carrying on something awful. When the hearse came to take him away, she screamed, such screaming I never did hear in all my born days. I thought she'd bust a blood vessel. She called someone on the telephone and kept shouting things about a girl named Evelyn. It was fierce."

"Didn't the doctor give her a sedative?"

"Some pills he gave her. *Pills.* Pills is a pretty poor substitute for a son." She opened the door wider and Blackshear stepped into the hall. "I'll go up and tell her. I don't guarantee she'll come down, though. What can you expect, at a time like this?"

"Has Miss Clarvoe arrived yet?"

"*Miss* Clarvoe?"

"Douglas' sister."

"I didn't even know he had a sister. Fancy that, no one mentioning a sister."

"She should be arriving any minute now," Blackshear said. "By the way, when she comes, you needn't let on that she isn't mentioned around here."

"As if I'd do a thing like that. Will she be staying, I mean, sleeping and eating and so forth?"

"I'm not sure."

"Well, it's a queer household, make no mistake about that."

"I won't."

"You can wait in the drawing room, if you like."

"I prefer the den."

"I'll show you . . ."

"I know the way, thanks."

The den smelled of last night's fire, and the morning rain. Someone had started to clean the room and been interrupted; a vacuum cleaner was propped against the davenport, and a dust cloth and a pile of unwashed ashtrays were sitting on the piano bench. The glass door that led out to the flagstone patio had been slid back and the November wind rustled across the floor and spiraled among the ashes in the fireplace.

Verna Clarvoe came in, her step slow and unsteady as if she was wading upstream in water too deep, against a current too strong. Her eyes were swollen almost shut, and there were scratches around her mouth as if she'd clawed herself in a fury of grief.

She spoke first. "Don't say you're sorry. Everyone says they're sorry and it doesn't matter, it doesn't *matter* whether they're sorry or not." She slumped into a chair. "Don't look at me. My eyes, they always get like this when I cry. I've forgotten where I put my drops. It's so cold in here, so *cold*."

Blackshear got up and closed the door. "I talked to Helen. She offered to come home."

"Offered?"

"Yes, offered." It was true enough. He hadn't suggested it. "She should have been here half an hour ago."

"She may have changed her mind."

"I don't think so."

"Why didn't she come with you?"

"I had some business to attend to first. It concerns you, Mrs. Clarvoe. If you're feeling well enough, I think I'd better tell you about it now."

"I feel all right."

"Terola is dead."

"Good."

"Did you hear what I said, Mrs. Clarvoe?"

"You said Terola is dead. I'm glad. Very glad. Why should you be surprised that I'm glad? I hope he suffered, I hope he suffered agonies."

"He didn't. It happened pretty quickly."

"How?"

"Someone stabbed him with a scissors."

"Someone murdered him?"

"Yes."

She sat, quiet, composed, smiling. "Ah, that's even better, isn't it?"

"Mrs. Clarvoe . . ."

"He must have been scared before he died, he

must have been terrified. You said he didn't suffer. He must have. Being scared is suffering. A scissors. I wish I'd seen it happen. I wish I'd been there."

"And I wish," Blackshear said, "that you could prove you weren't."

"What a silly remark."

"Perhaps, but it had to be made."

"I told you on the phone, I started out to see Terola but I changed my mind and came back."

"How far did you get? As far as the studio?"

"Yes."

"But you didn't go in."

"No. The place looked so squalid. I lost my nerve."

"Did you get as far as the door?"

"No. I never left the car. There's a yellow curb in front of the place, I just stopped there for a while."

"For how long?"

"A few minutes."

"Did anyone see you?"

"I was there, people must have seen me."

"What kind of car do you drive?"

"A black Buick sedan, last year's. There are hundreds like it, if that's what you're getting at."

"It is."

"Well, I didn't race up in a flame-red Ferrari.

There's no reason why anyone should have paid any particular attention to me."

"Let's hope no one did."

"What if they did?"

"If they did," Blackshear said patiently, "you'll probably be questioned by the police. You had a pretty good reason for hating Terola."

"If I killed everyone I hated, people would be dying like flies all over town."

"I don't believe that, Mrs. Clarvoe."

"Oh, stop. Stop that boy-psychiatrist approach. You don't know me. You don't understand. I'm filled with hatred. How can I help it? I've been cheated, duped, tricked—what do you expect? Everyone's let me down, everyone. Harrison, Douglas, they're out of this mess of a life. I'm the one that's left, always the one that's left."

From the driveway came the squeal of a car's moist brakes. They both heard it simultaneously, Verna with dread, Blackshear with relief. He hadn't admitted even to himself that he'd been worried about Helen's delayed arrival.

"That must be Helen now," Verna said. "I don't know what I'll say to her, how I'll act. We've been apart for so long, we're strangers."

"Then act like strangers—they're usually polite to each other, at least."

Blackshear went to the glass door and looked out across the patio toward the driveway. A woman was paying off the cab driver, a plump gray-haired woman in a black-and-white suit. When the cab backed out toward the street, she stood for a moment staring at the house as if she wasn't sure it was the right one. She saw Blackshear and appeared to recognize him. Instead of going to the front door she started across the patio toward the den with quick, aggressive strides.

Sensing trouble, Blackshear went out to meet her, closing the glass door behind him.

"Hello, Mrs. Merrick."

Her face was stiff and hostile. "Is she in there?"

"Yes."

She tried to brush past him but he reached out and clasped her arm and held it.

"Wait a minute, Mrs. Merrick."

"The sooner this is done, the better. Let go of my arm."

"I will, after you tell me what you have in mind."

"You mean, am I going to strangle the little bitch? No. Much as I'd like to."

He released her arm but she didn't move away from him. "Much as I'd like to," she repeated. "The things she said about Evelyn—incredible, terrible things. I can't, I won't, let her get away with it. No mother would."

"When did she make these remarks?"

"Less than an hour ago. She called me at the office—at the office, mind you; God knows who heard her, she was shouting so loud. She made the most terrible accusations against Evelyn. I can't even repeat them, they were so vile. She kept shouting something about giving Evelyn a dose of her own medicine. I don't know what she meant. Evelyn's always been so nice to her. Then she said that Evelyn was a murderer, that she murdered Douglas. I hung up, but she called back right away. I had to take the call, there were other people around. When she finally finished, I asked the boss for the rest of the morning off and here I am. I've got to get to the bottom of this."

"Isn't it rather a bad time?"

"It's a bad time, but it's not going to get any better. I have to find out why she said those things about Evelyn. If she's crazy with grief over Douglas, well, all right, I can undersand that, I've had a few griefs of my own. But why should she take it out on Evelyn of all people? My daughter has never hurt anyone in her life, it's so *unfair* that she should be attacked like this. She isn't here to defend herself, but I am. I'm here. And don't try and stop me this time, Mr. Blackshear. *I'm going to see Verna Clarvoe.*"

He watched her go into the house.

The two women faced each other in silence for a long time.

"If you've come for an apology," Verna said finally, "you won't get one. A person isn't obliged to apologize for telling the truth."

"I want an explanation, not an apology."

"You have the explanation."

"You've said nothing yet. Nothing."

"I gave Evelyn back some of what she gave me. The truth." Verna turned away, pressing her fingertips against her swollen eyelids. They felt hot, as if they'd been scalded by her tears. "She called me last night. She was quite friendly at first, she said I'd always been kind to her and she wanted to do me a favor in return. Then she told me about Douglas, the kind of life he was leading, the friends he had—sordid terrible things, in words so vile I don't see how a girl like Evelyn would know them, let alone speak them. That's your explanation, Mrs. Merrick."

"You can't be talking about Evelyn. Not *my* Evelyn."

"Why not?" Verna said, through clenched teeth. "She was talking about *my son*."

"I don't believe it. Evelyn would never do such a thing. She felt vindictive, perhaps, for a time after the marriage, but she's all over that. She has no hard feelings now. You saw that for yourself when you met us yesterday. She was pleasant and friendly, wasn't she? Wasn't she nice to you? You said yourself she bears no grudge."

"I am not arguing. I am too tired to argue. I told you what happened."

"You must be mistaken." Mrs. Merrick's plump face was like rising dough. "At least admit the possibility that you're mistaken."

"There's no such possibility."

"What time did she—what time was the call?"

"About ten."

"There. You see? You're wrong. Evie stayed with some friends last night. They had tickets for a play at the Biltmore Bowl."

"It was Evelyn who called me. I recognized her voice. And no one else, no woman, anyway, would know such things about Douglas."

"These things—how can you be sure they were true?"

"Because he admitted them, my son admitted them. And then he killed himself." She began to sway back and forth, her arms hugging her scrawny breasts. "Dougie. Dougie is dead. It's his birthday. We'd planned a little party . . . Oh God, go away, leave me alone."

"Mrs. Clarvoe, listen to me."

"No, no, no."

"I'd like to help you."

"Go away. My son is dead."

She left the way she had come, across the patio. Blackshear was waiting for her on the driveway, his suit collar turned up against the wind, his lips blue with cold.

He said, "I'll drive you back to work, Mrs. Merrick."

"No, thanks. You'd better go in to her." She began putting on her suede gloves. "At least Evelyn is alive. No matter what she's done, at least she's *alive*. That's enough to thank God for."

She turned and walked briskly into the wind, her head high.

CHAPTER 13

The wet patches on her dress, where she'd washed off the blood in the lavatory of the public library, were dry now, and it was safe to venture out into the street again. Even if the wind should blow her coat open, people wouldn't notice the faint stains left on her blouse, or if they did, they couldn't identify them.

She closed the book she'd been pretending to read for the past hour and returned it to the reference shelf. She knew no one in the library, and no one knew her. Still, it was dangerous to sit too long in any one place, especially a quiet place, because sometimes her mind clicked noisily like a metro-nome and spies could tell from its frequency what she was thinking.

One of these spies was an old man sitting at a table near the information desk, half-hidden be-hind a copy of *U.S. News and World Report.* How innocently engrossed he seemed, like a child gaz-ing at a picture book, but something about the angle of his head gave him away. She began to hum, quite loudly, so he couldn't hear her thoughts. He low-ered the magazine and gave her a sour look, realiz-ing that he'd been outwitted.

As she passed the table, she bent toward the old man and whispered, "It won't do you any good to follow me." Then she headed for the door, pulling her coat tight around her.

The victory was hers, of course. Still, the click-ing of her mind was becoming annoying. It came and went at odd moments, varying with the inten-sity of her thoughts, and if she was excited by an idea the noise was almost deafening, enough to drive her crazy.

Crazy. Not a word to use lightly. Terola had tried.

She walked quickly down the library steps and turned north, thinking of Terola. She'd been per-fectly nice to him, perfectly polite. He had had no reason to act as he did.

When he had answered the door he was wearing striped pajama bottoms and an undershirt.

"Hello, Mr. Terola."

"What do *you* want?"

"I just thought I'd pop in and . . ."

"Look, kid, pop out again, will you? I'm hung over."

He started to close the door but she was too quick for him. "I could make you some coffee, Mr. Terola."

"I've been making my own coffee for years."

"Then it's high time you tried mine. Where's the stove?"

Yawning, he led the way to the alcove and sat down on the edge of the day bed while she plugged in the hot plate and filled the coffee pot with water.

"How come the ministering angel act, kid?"

"I like to do a favor for a friend, now and then."

"And then the friend is supposed to do a favor right back at you?"

"That would be nice."

"What's the angle?"

"Those pictures you took of me," she said. "Burn them up."

"Why?"

"They didn't do me justice."

His eyebrows humped like black bushy caterpillars. "So?"

"So burn them up and take new ones. Good ones, the kind they hang in museums."

"Look, Elaine, Eileen, whatever your name is . . ."

"Evelyn."

"Look, Evelyn, you go home now like a good girl and I'll consider your proposition."

"You don't mean it."

"Sure, sure I do." He lay down on the bed and pulled the covers up to his waist.

"Do you promise, Mr. Terola?"

"Promise what?"

"To make me immortal."

"You crazy or something?" he said, punching the pillow irritably. "People hear you talking like that, they'll haul you off to the loony bin."

"Mr. Terola . . ."

"Blow, will you? I'm tired. I had a big night."

"Mr. Terola, do you think I'm pretty?"

"Gorgeous," he said, closing his eyes. "Just gorgeous, sweetheart."

"You're making fun of me."

"No, I'm not. Why should I make fun of you? Now blow, like a good girl, Eileen."

"Evelyn," she said. *"Evelyn."*

"All right. Sure."

"Say it. *Say Evelyn.*"

He opened his eyes and saw her standing over

him. "What's the matter with you, kid? Are you crazy?"

Crazy. Not a word to use lightly.

As she turned the next corner she looked back toward the library. The spy, disguised as an old man, was standing on the steps watching her, with the *U.S. News and Report* tucked under his arm. She began to run.

The old man went back into the library and stopped at the information desk where a red-haired girl sat surrounded by telephone directories from all over the country.

The girl smiled and said, "Here I thought you were running off with one of our magazines again, Mr. Hoffman."

"Not this time. Did you happen to notice the young woman who just left? The one with the dark coat?"

"Not particularly. Why?"

"I've been observing her for the past half-hour. Very peculiar, she seemed to me."

"We get a great many peculiar people in here," the girl said cheerfully. "Public institution, you know."

"I thought perhaps—well, the fact is, I couldn't help noticing she had stains on the front of her dress."

"She probably had spaghetti for lunch. You know how it dribbles."

"All the time I was watching her she kept a book open in front of her but she wasn't reading. A book on birds, I believe, though my eyes aren't what they used to be. Then, as she was leaving, she leaned down and whispered something to me. I didn't quite catch it. Odd, wouldn't you say?"

"Rather."

"I was wondering if I should, perhaps, report it to the police?"

"Now there you go again, Mr. Hoffman, imagining things!"

Because of the clicking of her mind and the danger of spies, she tried never to go into the same bar twice, but it was difficult to tell one from another, they were so similar. It was as if the decorations, the neon signs, the furniture, the customers, the bartenders, had all come from the same warehouse in a package deal.

The important difference was the location of the pay phone. At the Mecca it was in the rear, near the entrance to the men's room and cut off from the view of the people at the bar by a massive tub of philodendron.

With the folding door of the phone booth shut tight, she felt safe and warm and secluded, beyond

the reach of society, like a child in a playhouse
or a poet in an ivory tower.

She dialed, smiling to herself, breathing the
stale air deeply into her lungs as if it were pure
oxygen. Crestview 15115. As she waited for an
answer, she totaled the numbers. Thirteen. Add
one and divide by two, that made seven. Everything
had to make seven. Most people didn't know this,
and even when they were told, exhibited skepticism
or frank disbelief.

On the fifth ring (plus two) a woman's voice
said, "Hello."

"Is this the Clarvoe residence?"

"Yes."

"Mrs. Clarvoe?"

"She's not in."

"But I recognize you, Mrs. Clarvoe."

A sharp sound came over the wire, like a metal-
lic object striking the floor. "Who . . . Is that
you, Evelyn?"

"Didn't you expect to hear from me again?"

"Yes. Yes, I expected to."

A pause at the other end of the line, then a
flurry as if people were moving about, and a man's
voice, low and hurried, but distinct: "Ask her
about Helen. Ask her where Helen is."

"Who's that with you?" Evelyn said. As if she
didn't know. Poor old bungling Blackshear, looking

for her all over town, like a blind man feeling his
way through a forest. One of these days I will pop
out at him from behind a tree.

"No one's with me, Evelyn. There was, but I—
I sent him away. I felt you—you and I could talk
better alone. Evelyn? Are you still there?"

Still there. Safe, warm, secluded, the poet in the
playhouse, the child in the ivory tower.

A man, barrel-chested, bald, passed the phone
booth, and she peered out at him through the dirty,
narrow glass door. But he didn't even notice her.
His mind was on other things.

"Evelyn? Answer me. *Answer me.*"

"Well, you needn't shout," Evelyn said coldly.
"I'm not deaf, you know. I have what you might
call 20-20 hearing."

"I'm sorry I—shouted."

"That's better."

"Listen to me, please. Have you seen Helen?
Have you talked to her?"

"Why?" She smiled to herself because she
sounded so sober and earnest when all the time
she was bursting with laughter. Had she seen
Helen? What a marvelous joke. Prolong it. Draw
it out. Make it last a bit. "Why do you want to
know about Helen, Mrs. Clarvoe?"

"She was due here hours ago. She said she was
coming home."

"Oh, that."

"What do you mean? Have you . . . ?"

"She changed her mind. She didn't really want to come home anyway. She didn't want you to see her in her present condition."

"What is her—condition?"

"I promised not to tell. After all, we were friends once, and I ought to keep a promise to a friend."

"Please. For God's sake . . ."

"You keep shouting. I wish you wouldn't."

"All right," Verna whispered. "I won't shout. Just tell me, where's Helen and what's the matter with her?"

"Well, it's a long story." It wasn't really. It was short and sweet, but Mrs. Clarvoe must be taught a lesson. It was rude to shout.

"Evelyn, please, I beg of you . . ."

"No one has to beg me for the truth. I give it freely, don't I?"

"Yes."

"Whatever else people say about me, I'm not a liar."

"No. Of course not. You're not a liar. About Helen, she's all right, isn't she?"

"I don't know."

"But you said . . ."

"I didn't say she was all right or all wrong. All I

said was that she changed her mind, she's not coming home."

"Where is she?"

The barrel-chested man passed again, on his way back to the door. He had glass eyes and wooden lips.

"She's working," Evelyn said, "in a call house."

She had begun to tremble in excitement and anticipation, waiting for Verna's reaction, shock, disbelief, protest. None came.

"Did you hear me, Mrs. Clarvoe? Helen's working in a call house. It's down on South Flower Street. No place for a lady, I can tell you. But then, Helen never wanted to be a lady. A little excitement, that's what she needs. She'll get it, too. Oh my, yes. She'll get it."

Still no answer, not even the click of the receiver. The excitement began to spill out of her, like blood from a severed artery. She stuffed words into the wound to stem the flow.

"I got her the job. I met her outside her hotel this morning. She said she was sick of the idle life she was leading, she wanted to have something interesting to occupy her time. So I said I knew of something. Come with me, I said. And she came."

"Now I know you're lying," Verna said flatly. "Helen would never have gone anywhere with you. She's been warned."

"Warned? About me?"

"What have you done with her?"

"I told you, I got her a job."

"That's preposterous."

"Is it?" She hung up softly.

It was preposterous, nothing could be more preposterous than poor old Helen in a call house. Yet it was true.

She began to laugh, not ordinary laughter, but sounds with claws that tore at her chest and at the tissues of her throat. Burning with pain, she stumbled out into the street.

CHAPTER 14

During classes she was known as Dr. Laurence, but after five she was Claire and she lived near the U.C.L.A. campus in Westwood with her husband, John, and an overweight spaniel called Louise. She was a tall, well-built young woman with long beautiful legs and black hair which she wore in a coronet of braids. The style was old-fashioned and not particularly becoming, but it made her look unique, and she was well aware that this was about as much as she could expect with her limited equipment.

Frank, intelligent and unpretentious, she got on well with her students and had a great many

friends, most of them university people. Her closest
friend, however, had nothing to do with the faculty.

She had met Evelyn Merrick about eight months
previously on a double date with one of John's fra-
ternity brothers. On the way home she asked John,
"Well, how do you like her?"

"Who?"

"Evelyn Merrick."

"She's O.K.," John said.

"You certainly are enthusiastic."

"Thank God *one* of us doesn't form snap judg-
ments of people."

"Snap judgments are the only valid ones."

"How so?"

"Otherwise you get to like people just because
they satisfy a need in you and not because of their
intrinsic worth."

"Don't look now but your Ph. D. is showing."

"Let it show," Claire said. "I'll bet she's suffered.
And don't say *who* again. You know perfectly well
who."

"Most of us suffer here and there."

"I don't think it was here and there with Eve-
lyn. It seems to me that she's had a tremendous
shock of some kind, and not too long ago, either."

"Maybe she had shock treatments."

"You meant that to be funny, I suppose."

"Very, very slightly funny."

"As a matter of fact, I've seen people after they've had shock treatments, and they often show the same kind of wary attitude. Even if they hear a question the first time, they like to have it repeated. Things like that."

"So you think your new friend is a parolee from Camarillo."

"I think nothing of the sort," Claire said briskly. "My opinion is that she's suffered a shocking experience. I wonder what it could have been."

"Well, if I know you, angel, you'll have the whole story out of her the second time you meet."

He was wrong. During the next few months the two women met quite frequently, sometimes accidentally, since they lived only eight blocks apart, and sometimes by arrangement, for lunch or dinner or an early movie; but whatever Evelyn's shock had been, she didn't mention it, and any hints that Claire put out or direct questions she asked, were met with silence or a gentle remonstrance. At first, Evelyn's ability to keep a secret tantalized and annoyed Claire, but in time she came to respect it.

When John, who taught in the biology department, had to go away on field trips, Evelyn frequently came over to spend the night because Claire was nervous about being alone.

John liked to tease his wife about these occasions. "Afraid of the dark, at your age and weight."

"I can't help it."

"What did you do before you were married?"

"Before I was married, I lived in an apartment house with people below me, above me, and on both sides of me. The walls were so thin you could hear a pin drop, so there wasn't much chance of being murdered in your bed. It's quite different living in a house, like this. You're cut off from people."

"By a driveway and two flower beds."

"No, you know what I mean."

He knew exactly what she meant. She'd been brought up in a large family and lived in dormitories at school. There had always been people around, brothers and sisters, and friends and cousins and cousins of cousins. Being left in a house by herself made Claire feel insecure, and John was grateful to Evelyn for keeping her company in his absence. He had long since lost his original distrust of Evelyn and he believed now that, in her quiet way, she was just about the nicest girl in the world.

On Wednesday morning John took some of his freshmen students on a field trip to Los Padres National Forest and in the late afternoon Evelyn came over to the house to have dinner with Claire and spend the night. The two women had planned on going to see a play at the Biltmore Bowl but the arrangements were canceled when Claire arrived home with a severe cold. She went to bed at eight, drugged with antihistamines and codeine, and slept around the clock.

She woke up the next morning to the sound of dishes rattling and the smell of burning bacon. Slipping on her husband's old paisley bathrobe, she went out into the kitchen and found Evelyn making breakfast.

Claire said, yawning, "I could eat a horse."

"You may have to. I just ruined the last of the bacon."

"I like it well-done."

"It isn't well-done, it's charred."

"Well, Johnny says everybody should eat a certain amount of carbon. It acts as a purifying agent."

"You're making that up."

"It sounds rather plausible, though, doesn't it?"

"I can tell you're feeling better this morning."

"Oh, I am. How about you?"

Evelyn turned, her face white and aloof. "Me? There was never anything wrong with me."

"You're looking rocky. If I didn't know you better, I'd say you'd been out on a binge."

"Binges aren't much in my line."

"I was just kidding. I didn't mean to offend you."

"I'm afraid I offend easily these days."

"I know you do. John and I—well, we've noticed, and we couldn't help wondering."

"Wondering what?"

"If you shouldn't get married."

Evelyn was silent.

"I mean," Claire said with awkward earnestness, "marriage is a wonderful thing for a woman."

"Oh?"

"It really is. I don't know why you're looking so amused. What's funny?"

"I'm afraid," Evelyn said, smiling, "you wouldn't understand."

On Thursday afternoon Claire arrived home from her classes a little earlier than usual, around four-thirty. It was already getting dark and she didn't notice the car parked at the curb until she let the cocker spaniel out. The dog streaked across the lawn toward the car and began pawing at the door.

A man wearing a gray felt hat leaned out of the window and said, "That's not doing the finish of my car much good."

"So I see." She picked up the squirming spaniel.

"You're Mrs. Laurence?"

"That's right."

"I'm Paul Blackshear. I called you at the University this afternoon."

"Oh, yes."

"Is Miss Merrick here?"

"Not yet. She will be, though. If you'd like to come inside and wait . . ."

"Thanks, I would."

She led the way across the lawn, feeling apprehensive about letting the stranger into the house and yet unable to think of an adequate reason or a polite way to get rid of him.

In the living room she turned on all four of the lamps and left the drapes open, and when Blackshear had settled himself on the davenport she sat down in a straight-backed chair at the opposite end of the room.

"My husband," she lied firmly, "will be home at any minute."

Blackshear gave her a quizzical look. "Good. I'll need all the help I can get."

"Help with what?"

"I am trying to find a woman. I have reason to believe that Evelyn Merrick knows where this woman is."

"You mean you think Evelyn helped her to disappear?"

"I mean that, yes, but not in exactly the same sense that you do."

"I don't understand."

"The woman's disappearance was involuntary."

Claire stared at him, her face pale and astonished, her clenched fists pressed against her thighs. "What are you—implying?"

"It's obvious, isn't it, Mrs. Laurence?"

"No, it's not obvious. Nothing is obvious. I'm confused. I don't understand."

"I don't understand either, but I'm trying to. That's why I'm here. The woman who disappeared is Helen Clarvoe, a friend of mine. She was also, at one time, a friend of Evelyn Merrick's."

"At one time. Does that mean they quarreled?"

"Let's say they lost touch. Until last Monday night. At that time Miss Merrick telephoned Helen Clarvoe at her hotel. I won't go into detail but I assure you it wasn't an ordinary call from one old friend to another. As a result of it, Miss Clarvoe asked me to try and find Evelyn Merrick."

"Why?"

"She was disturbed and frightened by Miss Merrick's remarks. During the course of the week I've discovered that unusual telephone calls are Evelyn Merrick's specialty. Some people, when they have a grievance, blow their top, some brood, some write crank letters. Evelyn Merrick telephones."

"Nonsense," Claire said sharply. "I don't believe it. Ev hates to talk on the phone. I should know, I'm her best friend."

"Look, Mrs. Laurence, there may be some things about this woman that even her best friend doesn't know because Miss Merrick herself may not know them."

"That's not possible. Unless she's—are you trying to tell me she's insane?"

"It's a form of insanity."

"What is?"

"Multiple personality."

Claire rose abruptly and began to pace the room. "Ev is my best friend. You're a stranger. You come here and tell me some monstrous things about her and expect me to believe them. Well, I can't. I won't. What right have you got to go around diagnosing people as multiple personalities?"

"The theory isn't mine. It was advanced as a possibility by Miss Merrick's own doctor. I talked to him this afternoon. Miss Merrick has already suffered two emotional disturbances, one after her parents were divorced and her father went east to live, and the other after the breakup of her own marriage last year."

"Marriage," Claire repeated. "Ev's never been married."

"It's a matter of record."

"She's never said a word to me about it. I—why, just this morning we were talking and I said something about marriage being good for a woman and she—well, it doesn't matter now."

"Go on, Mrs. Laurence. She what?"

"Nothing. She just smiled, as if I'd said something unintentionally funny."

"You did."

"It wasn't a happy marriage, then?"

"No."

"Who is the man?"

"Helen Clarvoe's brother, Douglas." Blackshear hesitated, feeling a sudden and acute distaste for the job he had to do. "The young man died this morning."

"Why do you say it in that particular tone?"

"I wasn't aware of my tone."

"I was. You sounded as if you thought Evelyn had something to do with the man's death."

"There's no question in my mind. And two men have died."

She was shaken but obstinate. "There must be some terrible mistake. Ev is the gentlest creature in the world."

"Perhaps the one you know is. The other . . ."

"There is no other!" But the strength had gone out of her. she slumped into a chair, the back of her right hand pressed against her trembling mouth. "How—how did her husband die?"

"He killed himself."

"And the other man?"

"He was stabbed in the throat with a barber's shears some time this morning."

"My God," she said. "My God." And her hand slid down to her throat as if to try to staunch an invisible flow of blood. "She'll be here any time. What am I going to do?"

"Nothing. Act as if nothing's happened."

"How can I?"

"You must. Helen Clarvoe's life may be at stake."

"There's no chance you've—made a mistake?"

"There's always that chance, Mrs. Laurence, but it's pretty small. When she called Mrs. Clarvoe about Helen this afternoon she made no secret of her identity, she was even proud of herself."

He told her the content of the telephone call. She listened in stunned silence, rubbing the same place on her neck over and over again.

Outside, the spaniel began to bark. Blackshear turned and looked out of the window. A young woman was coming up the walk, laughing, while the spaniel jumped around her in frenzied delight. As she reached the steps of the porch, she leaned down and put out her arms and the spaniel leaped up into them. Both the girl and the dog looked very pleased with themselves at this remarkable feat.

It was Blackshear's first sight of Evelyn Merrick, and he thought how ironic it was that he should see her like this, laughing, greeting a dog —*the gentlest creature in the world,* Claire Laurence had said.

He turned and looked back at Claire. There were

tears in her eyes. She brushed them away with the
back of her hand as she went to unlock the door.

"Did you see that, Claire? She finally did it,
jumped right up into my arms! John said he's been
trying to teach her that for years. How's your cold?"

"Much better, thanks," Claire said. "We have
company."

"Company? Good."

"Come in and meet Mr. Blackshear."

"Just a sec, I'll shed my coat."

When she came into the room she was smiling
slightly, but it was a guarded smile, as if she al-
ready suspected that the company wasn't the kind
she would enjoy. She had short dark hair and gray
eyes that borrowed a little blue from the shirtwaist
dress she was wearing. When Blackshear had first
seen her greeting the spaniel, she had seemed strik-
ingly pretty. Now her animation was gone and she
looked quite commonplace. When she shook hands,
her clasp was limp and uninterested.

Blackshear said, "I heard Mrs. Laurence call me
company. The term isn't quite accurate."

She raised her dark straight brows. "No?"

"I would like to ask you some questions, if I may,
Miss Merrick."

"You may. I may even answer them."

"Mr. Blackshear is trying to find a woman who

disappeared," Claire said. "I told him you probably don't know a thing about it." She caught Blackshear's warning glance and added, "I'll go and make some coffee."

When she had gone, Evelyn said lightly, "This sounds very intriguing. Tell me more. Is it anyone I know?"

"Helen Clarvoe."

"*Helen.* Good heavens, I think that's the last name in the world I expected to hear. You say she's disappeared?"

"Yes."

"That is odd. Helen just doesn't do that sort of thing. She's, shall we say, on the conservative side."

"Yes."

"Still, she's old enough to do what she likes and if she wants to disappear why should anyone try and find her?"

"I'm not sure she wanted to."

"Oh really?" She seemed amused. "Helen isn't quite as dull as she acts, you know. There may be a man involved."

"I doubt that."

"In any case, I don't see how *I* can help you, Mr. Blackshear. I'll try, though."

"Thank you."

"Fire ahead."

"Are you acquainted with South Flower Street, Miss Merrick?"

"South Flower? That's downtown, isn't it?"

"Yes."

"I suppose I've driven along it. It's not the kind of section I'm familiar with, however."

"How long is it since you've seen Helen Clarvoe?"

"Over a year."

"Have you talked to her on the telephone?"

"Of course not. Why should I? We have nothing to discuss."

"There's no bad feeling between you?"

"There's no feeling at all between us. Not on my side, anyway."

"You were good friends at one time."

"In school, yes. That," she added with a shrug, "was a long time ago."

"You married Helen's brother, Douglas."

"I wouldn't say married. We went through a ceremony. Do you mind if I ask *you* a question now?"

"Not at all."

"Where did you get all your information about me?"

"From your mother."

She looked genuinely amused. "I might have

guessed. Mother's a great talker. She bares her soul to the milkman or the boy who delivers the groceries. Unfortunately, she bares mine too."

"Have you seen Douglas recently, Miss Merrick?"

"No, I haven't seen him. I've talked to him, though."

"When?"

"He telephoned me last night."

"Here?"

"Yes. After Claire had gone to bed."

"How did he know you were here?"

"I presume he called the house first and mother gave him this number."

"Do you think that's likely, in view of the resentment she feels toward him?"

"He probably didn't give his name." She added with a touch of scorn, "I assure you *I* haven't been keeping in touch with him. As far as the Clarvoes are concerned, I've had it. They're a good family to stay away from."

"What was Douglas' reason for calling, Miss Merrick?"

"I don't know. It's the first time I've heard from him since the annulment. He sounded lonely and confused. I was a little of both, myself, so we talked. Mostly about old times, years ago when Helen and I were at school together and I used to go home with her for holidays and week-ends. Dougie, we called him then, and he was always tagging around after us, no matter how much we teased him. Even Helen was happy in those days. Funny how everything's turned out."

But she spoke with complete detachment, as if the Evelyn of those times had no connection with herself. Blackshear wondered when the split in her personality had begun. Perhaps it had been there from infancy and no one suspected. Or perhaps it had started during her teens, during the very times she'd been reminiscing about to Douglas, the "happy" days. It was possible that those were the "happy" days because she had already started on her flight from reality.

Of one thing he was almost certain, the split in her personality was complete. The woman he was talking to was unaware of the existence of her deformed twin. She remembered talking to Douglas on the telephone the previous night, and yet he knew that if he told her she had also talked to Mrs. Clarvoe, and in quite a different fashion, she would be incredulous and probably very angry. Nothing would be gained by antagonizing her. His job was to wait until the change occurred and the twin took over. Only the twin knew what had happened to

Helen Clarvoe and where she was now. South Flower Street was miles long and had more brothels than restaurants.

Even if it had been safe to do so, there was no way of precipitating the change in Evelyn Merrick because no one knew what caused it. It could be something external, a word, a smell, a sound, a chance phrase of music, or it could be something inside, a sudden chemical change in the body itself.

"It was funny," she said, "hearing from Douglas again. I expected to feel all sorts of resentment against him, but I didn't. Odd, isn't it, how people plan what they'll do and say in a certain situation and then when the situation actually occurs, they don't do any of the things they've planned."

"What did you plan?"

"To make him feel like a worm. But I knew as soon as I heard his voice that I didn't have to say anything. He feels worse than any worm."

"Miss Merrick, how did you spend the day?"

"Looking for a job."

"Any particular kind of job, such as modeling, for instance?"

"*Modeling.* What on earth would give you that idea?"

"You're a very pretty girl."

"Nonsense. Thanks just the same, but it really is nonsense. I want a job with a future."

"You haven't been home, then, all day today?"

"No."

"Have you seen your mother?"

"No. I tried to get her at the flower shop this afternoon but they told me she was taking the rest of the afternoon off."

"She went to see Mrs. Clarvoe."

"Verna? Why on earth would she do that?"

"Douglas died this morning."

Evelyn sat quietly, her eyes lowered, her hands folded on her lap. When she spoke finally her voice was clear and distinct: "The coffee must be ready by now. I'll get you a cup."

"Miss Merrick . . ."

"What do you expect me to say, that I'm sorry? I'm not. I'm not sorry he's dead. He's better off. I'm only sorry he wasn't happier while he was alive."

It was the kindest thing he'd heard anyone say about Douglas since his death.

She asked, "How did it happen?"

Blackshear explained the circumstances of Douglas' death, while she sat with her head half-averted, looking contemplative, almost serene, like a child listening to a story she'd heard a dozen times before.

When he had finished, she said with a sigh, "Poor Douglas. In some ways he was the best of the bunch, of the Clarvoes, I mean. He at least had some warmth in him. Directed toward the wrong people, perhaps, but at least it was there."

"Helen has it, too."

"Helen is cold to the very marrow of her bones."

A premonition of disaster struck Blackshear like a spasm of pain. He had a feeling that her remark was intended to be quite literal, that the woman was trying to tell him Helen was already dead.

"Miss Merrick, I will ask you again."

"Yes?"

"Have you seen Helen Clarvoe today?"

"No."

"Do you know where she is?"

"No."

"Do you know if she's alive?"

"No."

"Do you remember telephoning her at her hotel last Monday night around 10 o'clock?"

"I can't remember something that never happened," she said gently. "I wish I could help you, Mr. Blackshear, but I'm afraid I don't know any of the answers."

It's useless he thought, and turned toward the door. "Thank you for trying, anyway."

"You're welcome. When you find Helen, let me know."

"Why?"

"Auld lang syne or curiosity, you name it. I'll make a little bet with you, Mr. Blackshear."

"Such as?"

"When you do find her, I'll bet she has a man with her."

Anger rose in him like an overflow of bile, leaving a green and bitter taste on his tongue and a rawness in his throat. He couldn't trust himself to speak.

He opened the door and stepped outside. In spite of the lighted houses and the street lamps, the darkness seemed as impenetrable as a jungle.

CHAPTER 15

She opened her eyes and closed them again quickly because the light was so blinding, but in that instant she saw that she was in a small white room like a cubicle in a hospital and the enormous woman bending over her was dressed all in white like a nurse.

The woman said in a harsh tired voice, "She's coming to. Give her some more of that whiskey."

"If she's drunk already, what you want to give her more of the same for, Bella?"

"Shut up and do as I say. Nothing brings a drunk

around faster than the smell of another drink. Hand me the bottle, Mollie."

"O.K."

"Now hold her head up while I pour. Ha ha ha, sounds like a society tea, eh? Madame Bella poured."

Miss Clarvoe tried to protest. She did not want the whiskey; it burned like acid. She jerked her head to one side and began to scream, but a hand closed over her mouth.

"You don't want to do that, dear," the woman called Bella said quite softly. "Maybe you're seeing things, eh? Maybe little animals running around, eh? Just take a nip or two of this and they'll go away."

"No, no! I don't want . . ."

"What's the matter, dear? You tell Bella. Everybody tells Bella their troubles. Maybe you got a monkey on your back, eh, dear?"

Miss Clarvoe shook her head. She didn't know what the woman was talking about. There was no monkey on her back, no little animals running around.

"Tell Bella, dear."

"I can't tell, I don't know," Miss Clarvoe said, her voice muffled against the fleshy palm of the woman's hand. "Let me go."

"Certainly, dear, just so long as you don't scream.

I can't have you disturbing my other customers. A man comes in after a hard day at the office, he wants a nice quiet massage, he don't want to hear a lady screaming, it upsets him."

Customers. Massage. It wasn't a hospital, then, and the woman in white wasn't a nurse.

"No more carryings-on, eh, dear? Promise Bella."

"Yes. I promise."

Miss Clarvoe opened her eyes. She was lying on a couch, and at the foot of the couch a very pretty blonde girl with acne was standing with a bottle of whiskey in her hand. The other woman, Bella, was enormously fat; her flesh quivered at the slightest movement and her chins hung in folds against her swarthy neck. Only her eyes looked human. They were dark despairing eyes that had experienced too much and interpreted too little.

The mere exertion of talking made her pant, and when she removed her hand from Miss Clarvoe's mouth she pressed it against her own heart as if to reassure herself that it was still beating.

"That's good material in her coat," the blonde girl said. "Imported from Scotland, it says, see right there on the label?"

"You can get back on the job now, Mollie."

"I don't have any more appointments for to-night."

"Then go home."

"What if she starts kicking up a fuss again?"

"I can handle her," the fat woman said. "Bella can handle her. Bella knows what the trouble is. Bella understands."

"Yeah, sure," the blonde girl said with a contemptuous little smile. "I'll bet you do. Well, you can have it. *I* like the normal ones."

"Shut up, dear."

"I wonder what's so special about material imported from Scotland."

"Blow, dear, and close the door after you."

The blonde girl left and closed the door behind her.

Miss Clarvoe pressed her fingertips against her eyes. She couldn't understand what the two women had been talking about, none of it made sense to her. She felt nauseated and dizzy and her head ached just behind her left ear as if someone had struck her there.

"My head," she said. "My head hurts."

"Her head hurts yet, listen to that. Naturally your head hurts, dear. You've been hitting the bottle."

"No. I never drink, never."

"You were reeking of the stuff when I found you out cold on my doorstep. I was saying good-bye to one of our regular customers who came in for his treatment, and when I opened the door there you were, lying against it. Stiff, dear. But stiff."

"That's impossible. I don't drink."

"Just rinse your mouth out now and then, eh?" The fat woman was laughing, every inch of her was laughing, mouth, chins, belly, breasts. When she had finished she wiped the moisture from her face and neck with a handkerchief. "That's my trouble, I'm too jolly. I laugh too much. It makes me sweat. Oh, how I sweat, dear, it's just not human the way poor Bella sweats. How about another nip of whiskey, dear?"

"No. No!" Miss Clarvoe tried to get up, lost her balance and rolled over on to the floor. "I must—I must get home—they're waiting for me."

The fat woman put her hands under Miss Clarvoe's armpits and helped her to her feet. "Who's waiting for you, dear?"

"I—don't know."

"Well, if you don't know, there's no hurry, is there? Lie down for a bit. Bella will make you feel better."

"No, no." The fat woman's breath was hot against the back of her neck and smelled overpoweringly of aniseed. "I must . . . They're waiting." Someone was waiting for her, she knew that, but she couldn't remember who it was. The faces in her memory were blurred and indistinct, people were shadows, places were all alike. She leaned against the wall and said faintly, "May I—have some water?"

"Certainly, dear."

The woman brought her some water in a paper cup and watched her while she drank.

"Feeling better now, dear?"

"Yes."

"Your coat's dirty. Give it to me and I'll brush it off for you."

"No. No." She clutched the coat tightly around her body.

"Ah, you're one of the shy ones. Bella knows. Bella's been in this business for a long, long time. You don't have to be shy with Bella. By the way, who recommended me, dear?"

"I don't understand."

"How did you get my name?"

"I didn't. I don't know your name."

The fat woman stood very still. Her eyes, tucked away under folds of flesh, were dead and purple like grapes. "How come you picked my place?"

"I didn't. I didn't pick any . . ."

"We mustn't tell fibs, dear. Bella hates fibs, they stir her to anger. Who gave you my name?"

"No one."

"You just came here by a lucky accident, eh? Is that right, dear?"

"I don't remember," Miss Clarvoe whispered. "I can't remember—Evelyn . . ."

"Is that who you are, dear? Evelyn?"

"No. No! I was—I was with Evelyn. She brought me here. She said . . ." Miss Clarvoe paused, holding her hands against her trembling mouth.

"What did she say, dear?"

"She said I belonged here."

The fat woman nodded and smiled and rubbed her chins. "She's a discerning girl, that Evelyn, oh my, yes."

"I don't understand what she meant."

"Don't you, dear. Well, lie down and rest a bit and Bella will tell you later. Let me take your coat, dear. What sweet ankles you have. I used to have a well-turned ankle myself in the old days. Now I eat. I eat and eat because nobody loves me. Nobody loves Bella, she is fat as an elephant, yes, but she's smart. Give me your pretty little coat, dear."

Miss Clarvoe stood stiff with terror.

"I revolt you, eh, dear? Is that it? Bella revolts you?"

"Stay away from me."

"Or is it that you're just shy, dear?"

"You monstrous old slut," Miss Clarvoe said and lunged toward the door.

But the fat woman was there ahead of her. She stood with her back pressed against the door, her arms crossed on her enormous breasts.

"Bella hates to be called names, dear. It stirs her to anger."

"If you don't let me out of here, I'll scream. I'll scream until the police come."

Bella was quiet a moment, then she said bitterly, "I believe you would, you're a nasty piece if I ever saw one. Well, that's gratitude for you. . . . I take you in, I look after you, you lap up my good whiskey, I say pretty things to you, none of them true, of course. Your ankles are lousy, they're like pipestems. . . ."

"Open that door."

Bella did not open the door but she moved away from it, still talking, half to herself: "All the things I do for people, and what do I get in return? Dirty names and looks. Bella is human. Maybe she is as fat as an elephant, but she is human, she likes a little gratitude now and then. It's a wicked world, there's no gratitude in it. Get out of here, you nasty girl, get out. Bella is stirred to anger. Get out, get out."

But the nasty girl had already left, and she was talking to an empty room. She sat down heavily on the couch, one hand pressed against her heart. It was still beating, fluttering like a captive bird under smothering folds of flesh.

"People are no damned good," Bella said.

Helen Clarvoe couldn't run. Her legs felt weak, as if the muscles had atrophied from long disuse, and the pain in her head had become worse. When she tried to think, her thoughts melted and fused and only one stood out clearly and distinctly from the others: I must get away. I must escape. I must run.

It was not important where she ran to. She had no plan. She didn't even know where she was until she reached the corner and saw the street signs: South Flower Street and Ashworth Avenue. She repeated the names to herself, hoping they would form a pattern in her mind, but neither of the names meant anything to her, and the neighborhood was strange. She knew she had never seen it before just as she knew that she didn't drink. Yet she'd come here, had walked or ridden or been carried, and when she arrived she was drunk. *Stiff*, Bella had said, *but stiff. Naturally your head hurts, dear, you've been hitting the bottle.*

"I never drink," Miss Clarvoe said. "I never touch liquor. Someone must have poured it down my throat. Someone. Evelyn."

An old man waiting at the corner for the traffic

light to change looked at her over the top of his bifocals with interest and pleasure. He often talked to himself. It was nice to know other people did it, too.

Miss Clarvoe saw him looking and she turned away and color flooded her cheeks, as if he had caught a glimpse of her, naked.

"Heh, heh, heh," the old man said and shuffled across the street, his shoulders shaking with mirth. Even the young ones talked to themselves these days. It was the age of the atom. Madmen have taken over. "Heh, heh, heh."

Miss Clarvoe touched her face. It was burning with humiliation. The old man had seen her talking to herself, perhaps he'd seen more than that. Perhaps he'd been walking by when she came out of Bella's place and he knew all about what kind of place it was. She must get away from the old man.

Miss Clarvoe turned and began running in the opposite direction, her coat billowing behind her, her thin legs moving stiffly.

At the next corner she stopped, gasping for breath, and held on to a lamppost for support. The sign on the post read Figueroa Street. I am not lost, she thought. I know Figueroa Street, I will wait here on the corner until an empty taxicab comes along. But something in her mind, some sixth sense, warned her not to stand still, and she started out again. Not running. The running had attracted too much attention. She must be casual, ordinary. No one must find out that somewhere, along these streets, or other streets, she had lost the day. It was night. The day had gone, passed her by, passed without touching her.

She walked on, her head bent, as if she were searching the sidewalk and the gutters for her lost day. People passed, cars roared by, the night was filled with noise and light and movement, but Miss Clarvoe did not raise her head. *I must pretend*, she thought. *I must pretend not to know I'm being followed.*

If she was clever enough, if she could control her panic, she might be able to find out who it was. Bella? The old man who'd caught her talking to herself? One of Bella's friends? None of them had anything to gain by following her, not even money. She had lost her purse, along with the day.

A bus was unloading at the next intersection and she quickened her pace and mingled with the crowd that was getting off the bus. Secure for a moment, she looked back, peering through the moving jungle of faces. Only one face stood out among the others, pale, composed, half-smiling. Evelyn Merrick. She was standing in the shadowed doorway of a small TV repair shop, leaning idly against the plate-glass window as if she had just paused for a rest during an evening stroll. But Miss Clarvoe knew it was not an evening stroll, it was a chase, and she was the beast in view. She moved in sudden terror. The woman at the window also moved. For an instant, before fear blacked out all thought, Helen realized that the woman was her own image.

She turned and began to run across the street, blind and deaf and numb with panic. She did not even feel the impact of the car that struck her.

When she returned to consciousness she was lying against the curb and people were standing over her, all talking at once.

"Saw her with my own eyes, out she dashed . . ."

"Red light . . ."

"Drunk, for sure. You can smell it a mile away."

"Honest to God, I didn't *see* her!"

"Let's get out of here. I don't want to be called as a witness."

"Come on, Joe, come on. I just can't stand the sight of blood."

Blood, Miss Clarvoe thought. I'm bleeding, then. It's all come true, what she said to me the first night. She saw it in her crystal ball, I was to be in an accident, bleeding, mutilated.

"What's a little blood, you watch prize fights all the time, don't you?"

"Must of been drunk . . ."

"With my own eyes . . ."

"Somebody call an ambulance."

"The lady in the green hat went to phone her husband, he's a doctor."

A young man wearing a cabdriver's uniform took off his coat and tried to put it under Miss Clarvoe's head. She thrust it away and sat up painfully. "I'm all right. Leave me alone."

The words were muffled and indistinct but the young man heard them. "You're supposed to lie there until the doctor comes."

"I don't need a doctor."

"I took a course in first aid and it says that in the book. Keep the patient warm and . . ."

"I'm not hurt." She dragged herself to her feet and began wiping the moisture off her face with a handkerchief, not knowing which was blood and which was sweat from all the running she'd done.

The crowd began to disperse—the show was over, no one was killed, too bad, better luck next time.

Only the young man in the cabbie's uniform lingered on, looking fretful. "It wasn't *my* fault. Everyone could see it wasn't my fault. You dashed right out in front of my cab, didn't give me a chance to stop, craziest thing I ever saw in my life."

Miss Clarvoe looked back at the doorway of the shop where she'd seen Evelyn Merrick just before the accident. The girl had left. Or else she had stepped farther back into the shadows to wait. That was the game she played best, waiting in shadows, walking in the night, watching for the unwary.

The cabbie was still talking, aggrieved and belligerent. "Everyone could see I did the best I could. I stopped, didn't I? I tried to minister first aid, didn't I?"

"Oh stop it, stop it! There's no time for argument. No *time*, I tell you."

He stepped back looking surprised. "I don't get . . ."

"Listen to me. What's your name?"

"Harry. Harry Reis."

"Listen, Harry, I must get away from here. I'm being followed. She was—I saw her in that doorway over there a few minutes ago. She intends to kill me."

"You don't say." A faint derisive smile stretched his mouth. He didn't even glance back at the doorway she was pointing at. "Maybe you escaped from somewheres, huh?"

"Escaped?"

"Sure. Escaped. Climbed over the wires."

She shook her head in mystification. He seemed to be talking in riddles like the fat woman, Bella. Monkeys on the back, little animals running around, wires to climb over. They were all English words but Miss Clarvoe couldn't understand them. She thought, perhaps I am the foreigner, perhaps I have been out of touch too long; the language has changed, and the people. The world has been taken over by the Bellas, and the Evelyn Merricks and little men like Harry with sly insinuating smiles. I must get back to my own room and lock the door against the ugliness.

"I must . . ."

"Sure," Harry said. "Sure. Anything for a lady."

He led the way to his cab. Miss Clarvoe dropped the bloody handkerchief on the curb and followed him. She wasn't aware yet of any pain, only of a terrible stiffness that seemed to cover her entire body like a plaster cast.

She got into the back seat of the cab and pulled her coat close around her. She remembered the blonde girl in Bella's place asking what was so special about fabric imported from Scotland. Miss Clarvoe didn't know, and it seemed important for her to figure it out. There were sheep, plenty of sheep, all over the world, but perhaps the Scottish sheep had finer wool. Wool. Sheep. Blackshear. She had forgotten about Mr. Blackshear. He was miles and years away, she couldn't even recall his face except that it looked a little like her father's.

The inside of the cab was dark and warm and the radio was turned on to a panel discussion on politics. All of the people on the panel had very definite ideas, firmly spoken. All of them knew exactly where the day had gone and what to expect from the night.

Harry got in and turned the radio off. "Where to?"

"The Monica Hotel."

"You live there?"

"Yes."

"You been living there long?"

"Yes."

"All the time steady?"

"Yes."

She could tell he didn't believe her. What did he believe? What were the wires she was supposed to have climbed over? She had never seen Harry before, never, she was sure of that. Yet he acted as though he knew secrets about her, ugly secrets.

"I will pay you," she said. "I have money in my hotel suite."

"Yes, ma'am."

"I'll send the boy down with it."

"Yes, ma'am."

She knew from his tone that he didn't expect any money, that he was humoring her as he would any drunk or liar or madman who happened to be his passenger. The customer is always right.

The headlights of the car following shone into the rear-view mirror and Miss Clarvoe saw Harry's face for a minute quite clearly. It was young and pleasant and very, very honest. A nice open face.

No one would suspect what kind of mind lay behind it. The fat woman wore her malice and her miseries for all the world to see; Harry's were hidden underneath the youthful blandness of his face, like worms at the core of an apple that looks sound from the outside.

Yet even Harry, even apple-cheeked, wormy-brained Harry knew where his day had gone. She had lost hers, dropped it somewhere like a handkerchief and picked it up again, soiled, from the dirty floor of a slut.

"Harry."

"Yes, ma'am." His tone was still sardonically polite.

"What day is this?"

"Thursday."

Thursday. Douglas died this morning. Mr. Blackshear came to the hotel to tell me about it. I promised to go home and keep mother company. Mr. Blackshear offered to drive me, but I refused. I didn't want him to touch me again. I was afraid. I went and waited in front of the hotel for a cab. People kept passing, strangers, hundreds of strangers. I felt very nervous and upset. The people terrified me and I didn't want to go home and face mother and hear her carry on about poor dead Douglas the way she did about father. I knew what a dreadful show she would put on. She always does, but none of it's real.

Cabs kept passing, some of them empty, but I couldn't force myself to hail one. Then someone spoke my name and I turned and saw Evelyn Merrick. She was standing right beside me, smiling, very sure of herself. The strangers, the traffic, didn't bother her. She'd always liked crowds and people, the more the merrier. I held my head up high, pretending I was just as poised and confident as she was. But it didn't work. I could never fool Evelyn. She said, "Scared, aren't you?" and she took my arm. I didn't mind. I usually hate people to touch me, but somehow this was different. The contact made me feel more secure. "Come on, let's have a drink some place," she said.

Come on, let's have a drink, let's lose a day, let's drop a handkerchief.

"You say something, ma'am?"

"No."

"Like I told you, if you want to change your mind and go back . . ."

"Go back where?"

"Back where you came from."

"I don't know what you're insinuating," she said as calmly as possible. "I *am* going back where I came from. I live at the Monica Hotel. I have a permanent suite there and have had for almost a year. Is that clear to you?"

"Yes, ma'am." His tone added, clear as mud. Harry had been around, he knew a thing or two, sometimes even three, and he was pretty certain that the woman had been playing around with narcotics, probably yellow jackets. She was obviously a lady and ladies didn't go in so much for heroin. Nembutal was more genteel both to use and to procure. You didn't have to hang around a street corner or the back booth of a café waiting for your contact. You could get yellow jackets just sitting in a nice upholstered chair in some fancy doctor's office, telling how you were nervous and worn-out and couldn't sleep.

Sleep wasn't always what they got, though. Sometimes the stuff went into reverse, and they did crazy things like taking off all their clothes in the middle of Pershing Park or racing up Sunset Boulevard at eighty miles an hour and fighting with the police when they were arrested. Ladies could sometimes behave worse than women.

He glanced back at Miss Clarvoe. She was crouched in the right-hand corner of the cab her arms pressed tautly across her chest, her lips moving slightly as if in prayer: She took my arm, I remember that, she took my arm like an old friend and said, *"Godiona gavotch."* It was our secret password in school when we were in trouble and needed help. "Godiona gavotch," I repeated, and suddenly it was as if the years had never passed, and we were friends back in school, giggling after the lights were out and plotting against the French mistress and sharing the treats from home. "Come and have a drink," she said. It was always like that. Evelyn was the one who initiated things, who formed the ideas and made the suggestions. I was the one who tagged along. I worshipped her, I wanted to be exactly like her, I would have followed her anywhere, like a sheep, the goat, the victim. I was marked, even then, and the marks have not faded with the years but have grown more distinct. Even Harry knows. He looks at me with contempt and his voice drips with it.

Apple-cheeked Harry, I see your worms.

"You want to go in the front or the back, ma'am?" Harry said.

"I am not in the habit of using a service entrance."

"I just thought, being you were messed up a little . . ."

"It doesn't matter." It did matter, she wanted nothing more than to go in the back entrance and sneak up to her room unnoticed, but it was impossible. Her keys had been in the purse she'd lost. "About the fare, I'll send a bellboy down with the money. How much is it?"

"Three dollars even." He stopped the cab at the marquee of the hotel but he made no move to get out and open the door for her. He didn't expect a tip, he didn't even expect the fare, and for once it didn't matter much to him. She was a creepy dame, he wanted to see the end of her.

Miss Clarvoe opened the door for herself and stepped out onto the sidewalk and pulled her collar up high to hide the wound under her ear. The torn stockings, the rip in her coat, she couldn't hide; she could only move as rapidly as possible through the lobby, trying to outrun the stares of the curious.

Mr. Horner, the elderly desk clerk, was busy registering some new guests, but when he saw Miss Clarvoe he dropped everything and came over to her, his eyes bulging and his mouth working with excitement.

"Why, Miss Clarvoe. Why, Miss *Clarvoe*, for goodness sake . . ."

"I lost my keys. May I have a duplicate set, please?"

"Everybody's been looking for you, Miss Clarvoe. Just everybody. Why, they . . ."

"They need look no further."

"But what happened to you?"

She answered without hesitation. "It was such a nice day I decided to take a little trip into the country." Had it been a nice day? She didn't know.

She couldn't remember the weather of the day any more than she could its contents. "The country," she added, "is very beautiful this time of year. The lupine is in bloom, you know. Very lovely." The lies rolled glibly off her tongue. She couldn't stop them. Any words were better than none; any memory, however false, was better than a blank. "Unfortunately, I tripped over a boulder and tore my coat and my stockings." As she talked the scene came into sharper focus. Details appeared, the shape and color of the boulder she'd fallen over, the hills blue with lupine and dotted with the wild orange of poppies, and beyond the hills the gray-green dwarfs of mountains with their parched and stunted trees.

"You should," Mr. Horner said with reproach, "have let someone know. Everyone's been in a tizzy. The police were here, with a Mr. Blackshear."

"Police?"

"I had to let them into your suite. They insisted. There was nothing I could do." He leaned across the desk and added in a confidential whisper, "They thought you might have been kidnapped by a maniac."

Color splashed across Miss Clarvoe's face and disappeared, leaving her skin ashen. Kidnapped by a maniac? No, it wasn't like that at all. I went with an old friend to have a drink. I was frightened and confused by all the strangers and the traffic, and she rescued me. She put her hand on my arm and I felt secure. By myself I was a nothing, but with Evelyn there beside me I could see people looking at us with interest and curiosity, yes even admiration. "Come and have a drink," she said.

I could have stood there forever, being looked at, being admired—it is a wonderful feeling. But Evelyn likes excitement, she wanted to be on the move. She kept saying, come on, come on, come on, as if she had some very intriguing plan in mind and wanted me to share it. I said, "I promised to go home and stay with mother because Douglas is dead." She called each of them an ugly name, mother and Douglas, and when I looked shocked she laughed at me for being a prude. I've never wanted to be a prude; I've simply never known how to be anything else. "I've got a friend," Evelyn said. "He's a lot of fun, a real joker. Let's go over and have some laughs."

Douglas was dead, my own brother; I shouldn't have felt like laughing, and yet I did. I asked her who the friend was who was such a joker and I remember what she answered. It's odd how the name has stuck in my mind when I've forgotten so many other things. Jack Terola. "He is an artist with the camera," Evelyn said. "He's going to take pictures of me that will be shown all over the country. He's going to make me immortal." I felt the knife of envy twisting in my heart. I wanted to be immortal, too.

"I had to co-operate with the police," Mr. Horner said. "I didn't have any choice. It was a question of handing over the keys to your suite or having them taken from me."

"I dislike the idea of anyone prying into my personal affairs."

"Everyone acted in your best interests, Miss Clarvoe."

"Indeed."

"After all, anything might have happened."

"What happened," she said coldly, "is that I went into the country with a friend of mine."

"Ah, yes. To see the lupine in bloom."

"That's correct."

Mr. Horner turned away, his lip curling slightly. It was November. The lupine wouldn't be in bloom for another three or four months.

He returned with the duplicate set of keys and laid them on the desk. "There are some messages for you, Miss Clarvoe. You are to call Mr. Blackshear immediately; he is at your mother's house."

"Thank you."

"Oh yes, and someone asked me to put this note in your box. A young lady."

The note was written in an ostentatious backhand on hotel stationery which had been folded twice:

*I am waiting in the lobby. I must see you at once.
Evelyn Merrick.*

She wanted to run but her legs ached with weariness; they would not carry her father. She'd already run too far, too fast, down too many strange and terrifying streets.

CHAPTER 16

She turned and saw Evelyn Merrick coming toward her across the lobby, picking her way fastidiously through the crowd. The day, which had changed Miss Clarvoe, had changed Evelyn too. She wasn't smiling and self-assured as she'd been when they met on the street. She was a grim-faced, cold-eyed stranger, dressed all in black as if in mourning.

"I see you got my note."

"Yes," Miss Clarvoe said, "I have it."

"We must have a talk."

"Yes." Yes, we must. I must find out how I lost

the day, how the minutes passed overhead without touching me, like birds in a hurry. Wild-geese minutes. I remember father took us hunting once, Evelyn and me. Father was angry with me that day because the sun gave me a headache. He said I was a spoilsport and a crybaby. He said, *"Why can't you be more like Evelyn?"*

"Everyone's been worried about you," Evelyn said. "Where have you been?"

"You know, you know very well. I was with you."

"What are you talking about?"

"We went into the country together—to see the lupine—we . . ."

The stranger's voice was harsh and ugly. "You've always told fantastic lies, Helen, but this is going too far. I haven't seen you for nearly a year."

"You mustn't try to deny it. . . ."

"I'm not *trying* to deny it. I am denying it!"

"Please keep your voice down. People are staring. I can't have people staring. I have a reputation, a name, to protect."

"No one is paying the least attention to us."

"Yes, they are. You see, my stockings are torn, and my coat. From the country. You have forgotten how we went into the country, you and I, to see the lupine. I tripped over a boulder and fell." But her voice trailed upward into a question mark, and her eyes were uncertain and afraid. "You—you remember now?"

"There's nothing to remember."

"Nothing?"

"I haven't seen you for nearly a year, Helen."

"But this morning—this morning you met me outside the hotel. You asked me to have a drink with you, you said you were on your way over to see a man who would make you immortal and you wanted me to come along."

"It doesn't even make sense."

"Yes, yes, it does! I even remember the man's name. Terola. Jack Terola."

Evelyn's voice was quiet, insistent. "You went to see this man Terola?"

"I don't know. I think we—we both went, you and I. After all, I wouldn't go to such a place alone and beside Terola was your friend, not mine."

"I never heard the name before in my life. Until I read the evening papers."

"Papers?"

"Terola was murdered shortly before noon today," Evelyn said. "It's important for you to remember, Helen. Did you go there this morning?"

Miss Clarvoe said nothing, and her face was blank.

"Did you see Terola this morning, Helen?"

"I must—I must go upstairs."

"We have to talk."

"No. No, I must go upstairs and lock my door against all the ugliness." She turned, slowly, and began walking toward the elevator, her shoulders hunched, her hands jammed into the pockets of her coat as if she wanted to avoid all physical contact with other people.

She waited until one of the elevators was empty. Then she stepped inside and ordered the operator to close the door immediately. The operator, an old man, was no bigger than a child, as if the years he'd spent inside the tiny elevator had stunted his growth. He was accustomed to Miss Clarvoe's idiosyncrasies, such as riding alone in elevators, and he'd been well enough tipped, in the past, to indulge them.

He shut the door and as the elevator began to ascend he kept his eyes on the floor indicator. "A wintry day, Miss Clarvoe."

"I don't know. I lost mine."

"Beg pardon, ma'am?"

"I lost my day," she said slowly. "I've looked everywhere for it but I can't find it."

"Are you—are you feeling all right, Miss Clarvoe?"

"Don't call me that."

"Ma'am?"

"Call me Evelyn."

"Yes, ma'am."

"Well, say it. Go ahead. *Say Evelyn.*"

"Evelyn," the old man said and began to tremble.

Back in her suite she locked the door and without even taking off her coat she went immediately to the telephone. As she dialed, she felt the excitement rising inside her like molten lava in a crater.

"Mrs. Clarvoe?"

"Is that—that's you, Evelyn?"

"Certainly it's me. I've done you another favor."

"Please. Have mercy."

"Don't snivel, I hate that, I hate snivelers."

"Evelyn . . ."

"I just wanted to tell you that I've found Helen for you. I have her all locked up in her hotel room, safe and sound."

"Is she all right?"

"Don't worry, I'm looking after her. I'm the only one who knows how to treat her. She's been a bad girl, she needs a little discipline. She tells lies, you know, awful lies, so she must be taught a lesson or two like the others."

"Let me talk to Helen."

"Oh no. She can't talk right now. It isn't her turn. We have to take turns, you know. It's very inconvenient because Helen won't voluntarily give me my turn so I just have to go ahead and take it. She was feeling weak from the accident, and her head hurt, so I simply took over. I feel fine. I'm never sick. I leave that to her. All the sordid things like being sick or getting old, I leave to her. I'm only twenty-one; that old crock is over thirty. . . ."

Evelyn Merrick was waiting for Blackshear in the lobby when he arrived twenty minutes later.

"I got here as soon as I could," Blackshear said. "Where is Helen?"

"Locked in her room. I followed her up and tried to talk to her, but she paid no attention to my knocking. So I listened at the door. I could hear her inside."

"What was she doing?"

"You know what she was doing, Mr. Blackshear. I told you when I called you. She was telephoning, using my name, my voice, pretending to be me."

Blackshear was grim. "I wish that's all it was, a child's game, like pretending."

"What else is it?"

"She has a rare form of insanity, Miss Merrick, the disease I thought you had. A doctor would call it multiple personality. A priest might call it possession by a devil. Helen Clarvoe is possessed by a devil and she gives your name to it."

"Why should she do that to me?"

"Are you willing to help me find out?"

"I don't know. What must I do?"

"We'll go up to her room and talk to her."

"She won't let us in."

"We can try," Blackshear said. "All I seem able to do for Helen is try. Try, and fail, and try again."

They took the elevator up to the third floor and walked down the long carpeted hall to Miss Clarvoe's suite. The door was closed and locked. No light showed around its edges, but Blackshear could hear a woman talking inside the room. It was not Helen's voice, tired, uninterested; it was loud and brash and shrill, like a schoolgirl's.

He rapped sharply on the door with his knuckles and called out, "Helen? Let me in."

"Go away, you old fool, and leave us alone."

"Are you in there, Helen?"

"Look at the mess you've got me in now. He's found me. That's what you wanted, isn't it? You've always been jealous of me; you've always tried to cut me out of your life. Now you've done it, calling in that man Blackshear and the police to hunt me down like a common criminal. I'm not a common criminal. All I did to Terola was touch him with the scissors to teach him a little lesson. How was I to know his flesh was soft as butter? An ordinary man wouldn't even have bled, my touch was so delicate. It wasn't my fault the poor fool died. But the police won't believe that. I'll have to hide here with you.

Just you and me, how about that? God knows if I can stand it, you should be able to. You're dull company, old girl, you can't deny that. I may have to slip out now and then for a bit of fun."

Blackshear tried to call out again but the words died of despair in his throat: *Fight, Helen, Fight back. Stand up to her.* He began pounding on the door with his fists.

"Listen to that, will you? He's trying to break the door down to get to his sweetheart, isn't that touching? Little does he know how many doors he'll have to break down; this one's only the first. There are a hundred more and that pitiful idiot out there thinks he can do it with his fists. Funny boy. Tell him to go away, Helen. Tell him not to bother us. Tell him if he doesn't go away he'll never see you alive again. Go on. Speak. *Speak,* you ugly crone!"

. A pause, then Helen's voice, a tattered whisper, "Mr. Blackshear. Paul. Go away."

"Helen, hang on. I'm going to help you."

"Go away, go away."

"Hear that, lover boy? Go away, she says. Lover boy. God, that's funny. What a romance you had, eh, Helen? Did you *really* think anyone could fall in love with you, you old hag? Take a look in the crystal ball, you crow."

She began to laugh. The sound rose and fell, a siren screaming disaster, and then there was a sudden silence, as if the loud night were holding its breath.

Blackshear pressed his mouth against the crack of the door and said, "Helen, listen to me."

"Go away."

"Unlock your door. Evelyn Merrick is here with me."

"Liar."

"Unlock your door and you can see for yourself. You are not Evelyn. Evelyn is out here with me."

"Liar, liar, liar!"

"Please, Helen, let us in so we can help you. . . . Say something to her, Miss Merrick."

"We are not trying to fool you," Evelyn said. "This is really Evelyn, Helen."

"Liars!" But the lock clicked and the chain slid back and slowly the door opened and Miss Clarvoe's tormented face peered out. She spoke to Blackshear, her pale mouth working painfully to form the words: "Helen is not here. She went away. She is old and sick and full of misery and wants to be let alone."

"Listen to me, Helen," Blackshear said. "You are not old and sick. . . ."

"*I'm* not, no. *She* is. You're mixed up. I'm Evelyn. I'm fine. I'm twenty-one. I'm pretty, I'm popular, I have lots of fun. I never get sick or tired. I'm going to be immortal." She stopped suddenly, her eyes fixed on Evelyn Merrick, fascinated, repelled. "That girl—who is she?"

"You know who she is, Helen. She's Evelyn Merrick."

"She's an impostor. Get rid of her. Tell her to go away."

"All right," Blackshear said wearily. "All right." He turned to Evelyn. "You'd better go down to the lobby and call a doctor."

Miss Clarvoe watched Evelyn go down the hall and get into the elevator. "Why should she call a doctor? Is she sick?"

"No."

"Why should she call a doctor, then, if she isn't sick?" She added peevishly, "I don't much like you. You're sly. You're a sly old man. You're too old for me. Not much use your hanging around. I'm only twenty-one. I have a hundred boy friends. . . ."

"Helen, please."

"Don't call me that, don't say that name. I'm not Helen."

"Yes, you are. You're Helen, and I don't want you to be anybody else. I like you exactly as you are. Other people will, too, if you'll let them. They'll like you just as you are, just for yourself alone, Helen."

"No! I'm not Helen, I don't want to be Helen! I hate her!"

"Helen is a fine young woman," Blackshear said quietly. "She is intelligent and sensitive—yes, and pretty too."

"Pretty? That crock? That hag? That ugly crone?"

She started to close the door but Blackshear pressed his weight against it. She released the door and stepped backward into the room, one hand behind her back, like a child concealing a forbidden object. But Blackshear did not have to guess what she was concealing. He could see her image in the round mirror above the telephone stand.

"Put down the paper knife, Helen. Put it back on the desk where it belongs. You're very strong, you might hurt someone accidentally. . . . How did you meet Terola in the first place, Helen?"

"In a bar. He was having a drink and he looked over at me and fell in love with me at first sight. Men do. They can't help it. I have this magnetism. Do you feel it?"

"Yes. Yes, I feel it. Put down the knife, Helen."

"I'm not Helen! I am Evelyn. Say it. Say I'm Evelyn."

He stared at her, saying nothing, and suddenly she wheeled around and ran across the room to the mirror. But the face she saw in it was not her own. It was not a face at all, it was a dozen faces, going round and round—Evelyn and Douglas and Blackshear, Verna and Terola and her father, Miss Hudson and Harley Moore and the desk clerk and the little old man in the elevator—all the faces were revolving like a ferris wheel, and as they revolved, they moved their mouths and screamed out words *"What's the matter with you, kid, are you crazy?"* *"You've always told the most fantastic lies."* *"What a pity we didn't have a girl like Evelyn."* *"You can't make a silk purse out of a sow's ear."* *"Why can't you be more like Evelyn?"*

The voices faded into silence, the ferris wheel of faces stopped, and there was only one image left in the mirror. It was her own face, and the mouth that moved was her own mouth, and the words that came out were uttered by her own voice: "God help me."

Memory stabbed at her with agonizing thrusts. She remembered the bars, the phone booths, the running, the strange streets. She remembered Terola and the odd, incredulous way he looked just before he died and the acrid smell of the coffee boiling over on the stove. She remembered taking the bills from her own money clip and then thinking later that they'd been stolen. She remembered the cat in the alley, the rays from the night air, the taste of rain, the young man who'd laughed because she was waterproof. . . .

"Give me the knife, Helen."

In the mirror she could see Blackshear approaching, slowly and cautiously, a hunter with a beast in view.

"It's all right, Helen. Don't get excited. Everything's going to be all right."

A pause, and then he began to talk again in a low, persuasive voice, about doctors and hospitals and rest and care and the future. Always the future, as if it was definite and tangible, rosy and round like an apple.

She stared into the crystal ball of the mirror and she saw her future, the nights poisoned by memories, the days corroded by desire.

"It's only a matter of time, Helen. You'll be well again."

"Be quiet," she said. "You lie."

She looked down at the knife in her hand and it seemed to her that it alone could speak the truth, that it was her last, her final friend.

She pressed the knife into the soft hollow of her throat. She felt no pain, only a little surprise at how pretty the blood looked, like bright and endless ribbons that would never again be tied.

AFTERWORD

When *Beast in View* was about half-written, I happened to see on television a play which depressed me immeasurably because the plot was the same as the one I was writing. If the play had been poorly acted or badly written, its effect on me would have been minimized. But the actress was Geraldine Fitzgerald and the playwright was Gore Vidal. I decided to abandon my book.

At this point my husband, Ross Macdonald, stepped in as he often had in the past. His idea was elementary but it altered the whole book: Retain the split personality theme but make Helen Clarvoe's alter ego a real person. He saved the book from becoming what would have been by this time a cliché. Instead, it is something of a minor classic.

Beast in View without Evelyn Merrick? Unthinkable. My husband was a critic before he was a writer, and this has been a boon for both of us.

Thanks, Ross Macdonald. I would have done the same for you, but I couldn't do it and you didn't need it.

Margaret Millar

Santa Barbara, Calif.
February, 1983

ABOUT THE AUTHOR

Margaret Millar was born in Kitchener, Ontario, Canada, and educated at the Kitchener Collegiate Institute and the University of Toronto. In 1938 she married Kenneth Millar, better known under his pen name of Ross Macdonald, and for over forty years they enjoyed a unique relationship as a husband and wife who successfully pursued separate writing careers.

She published her first novel, *The Invisible Worm,* in 1941. Now, over four decades later, she is busily polishing her twenty-fifth work of fiction. During that time she has established herself as one of the great practitioners in the field of mystery and psychological suspense. Her work has been translated into more than a dozen foreign languages, appeared in twenty-seven paperback editions and has been selected seventeen times by book clubs. She received an Edgar Award for the Best Mystery of the Year with her classic *Beast in View;* and two of her other novels, *The Fiend* and *How Like an Angel,* were runners-up for that award. She is a past President of the Mystery Writers of America, and in 1983 she received that organization's most prestigious honor, the Grand Master Award, for lifetime achievement.